CINDERELLA
LIBERTY

CINDERELLA LIBERTY

A NOVEL BY

DARRYL

PONICSAN

HARPER & ROW, PUBLISHERS

NEW YORK, EVANSTON, SAN FRANCISCO, LONDON

The lines on pages 138 and 139 are adapted from "Lament" by Edna St. Vincent Millay. *Collected Poems,* Harper & Row Publishers, Inc. Copyright 1921, 1948 by Edna St. Vincent Millay.

FIRST EDITION

STANDARD BOOK NUMBER: 06–013402–X

LIBRARY OF CONGRESS CATALOG CARD NUMBER: 72–9767

In a San Juan bar we fought each other to buy her a champagne cocktail. *"Los marineros locos,"* she called us. This book is dedicated to *los marineros locos* of all countries.

1

JOHN BAGGS, yeoman second class, is a sailor with a very sore ass. Up before reveille, he eases it into a pan of steaming hot water on the deck of the deserted head. For diversion he watches the roaches as they scurry back and forth in front of him, unmindful of the forces that are stirring up the sea below them.

Baggs believes that roaches do not make the best of pets. They do not return love like dogs. They are too shy and elusive to be studied like fish. They do not sing like birds. On the other hand, like cats they can take care of themselves and have been doing so since long, long before man or cat grinned through his whiskers at the face of the earth.

Baggs dips his finger into his sitz bath and splashes a few drops of water at the roaches, just to remind them that life at sea was never meant to be without its perils.

Though not handsome, the roaches are clean and harmless creatures and have never bitten man in anger, often in spite of quite sound reasons to do so. For his part, man has not been able to find joy in the company of roaches, and the only pleasure he has had from them has been to step upon their brittle shells and hear them crunch like the first bite of a fresh Fifth Avenue.

A new sailor aboard ship soon gives up stepping on them because it seems only to increase their already vast numbers. Soon after reasonably lamenting the lie of *Oh, my, the Navy certainly does keep clean ships,* the new sailor learns to accept this larger crew as being in the same boat he is, and he eventually learns to greet them with grim good humor every morning when reveille sounds, like now.

The sound of the bosun's pipe slashes through the berthing compartment like a shrieking bird in panic, until it falls dead and the bosun himself yells, "Now, reveille, reveille! All hands up! Prepare to relieve the watch. Reveille! Reveille!"

A sailor crawls out of his rack and opens his locker. Ten of the little cuties dash away from the light, which they hate.

The nine roaches who have been feeding upon what nutrition clings to the sailor's blue trousers make for darker banquets, but the strongest, one who has staked rights to the goodies on the sailor's toothbrush, the sweetest meal, is loath to leave his prize. The sailor picks up the toothbrush, the roach boldly and greedily clinging to the bristles, and flicks it against his finger, sending his parasite through the air at a late sleeper. The roach lands near the sleeper's chin and digs like a spoiled puppy under the blanket to the dark warmth and security below.

In the head, John Baggs prepares himself for the onslaught.

The sailor who flicked away the roach takes toothbrush and douche bag and towel (that somehow has stayed damp throughout this Mediterranean cruise) and goes to the head with the others, all bumping each other and the bulkheads without comment or apology.

Though it is 0600 the temperature in the lower berthing spaces is already in the nineties and the bodies that go yawning and sweating into the head smell hot and gamy, but in the head few can notice, because the crappers are all in service, two facing rows of three each, without panels, so close that the knees of the men on one row almost touch the knees of the men on the other. Certainly if the men on opposite crappers care to, perhaps in closing a bet, they can shake hands. A metal bar runs along the front of each row, within reaching distance, and impaled on the bars are rolls of toilet paper, Navy shish kebab.

There is enough space between the rolls for sailors to grip the bar when indiscretion takes its revenge on the natural body functions.

The six men in turn and together break wind and lower their eyes and chins, seeking no championship in this unnegotiated competition. The ones who wait are in fair spirits, because usually two of the six crappers, and never the same two, are inoperative and hold their bounty to public view like flea market merchants until some poor seaman deuce, lower than whale shit, is given the repair detail. But today all systems are go and the wait should not be too long.

The smell of even this side of the head is cured by the desolate smell of salt that washes from bulkhead to bulkhead with the roll of the ship, half an inch deep and floating the proof that even sailors can become seasick.

There are three corridors in the head, all partially visible upon opening the door. The center is made up of two rows of metal washbasins. Behind them are two rows of urinals, so that you can simultaneously shave and converse with your mate who is taking a leak in front of you. If you are not too tall you can lower your face to the basin without bumping the man at the basin behind you, if he is not too tall.

To the left of center, a row of four shower heads, three of which work, again never the same three. The showers are, against design, also footbaths, because the one feeble drain is too slow a sucker and three inches of dirty, tepid water remains at one's feet until all showers are turned off.

To the right of center, the crappers, already described.

A sailor's morning toilette is no casual routine. There is no preening of the hair, brushing of the fingernails, squeezing of the pimples. There is no leisurely read of the *Reader's Digest*. The quicker you do your thing and get out, the better place you get in the chow line. The better your place in the chow line, the

3

better your chances of eating breakfast sitting down and the better your chances of eating chow that is hot, though when the sea is rough as it is today even hot chow is weird chow.

After waiting through a week of calm seas for fried eggs and then receiving them on the morning the water goes wild, a sailor can only believe it is part of the Great Naval Plan to give you what you want and then, incredibly, make sure you don't enjoy it.

You watch your eggs open onto the grill and watch them slide with the pitch of the ship, so that they are fried in the shape of a twelve-inch ruler.

With your arms wrapped around your tray to keep it from sliding off the mess table to the deck, you stare at the eggs and wonder should you eat them or save them for Salvador Dali. Hunger wins, as it must, and you pick up the egg by one end and eat it like a super noodle. You've lost your coffee in the process. When you instinctively bend over to pick up the pieces of the coffee cup, you lose the entire tray. You're not very hungry anyhow.

You are aboard the USS *Begonia* (APA-31); how could you have an appetite?

She was originally constructed as a passenger liner, which accounts for a few of her peculiarities: portholes, enclosed stairways, wooden banisters. Midway through construction her natural development was arrested by an endeavor of man we now know as World War II. No librarian from Oswego would ever find romance on her walkways. No newly married couple from Richmond would ever dance to melodic strains in her ballroom. No businessman from Peoria would ever swill champagne or lick caviar off his fingers in her staterooms.

She would become an instrument of destruction.

Nothing so grand, actually, as an instrument of destruction. The first gunner's mate to report aboard her looked at the guns she was fitted with, sneered, and asked how he could transfer off this chicken of the sea.

No one would tell him that she was constructed cut-rate with only one mission: to take a cargo of troops and equipment across the water. The thing was to get them to the action. She was expendable and it was assumed that she would be torpedoed, hopefully on the return trip when she was empty of anything valuable.

When she returned unscathed, the Navy smiled wryly yet paternally and sent her off again, already ahead of the game. When she returned a second time, they loaded her with more important cargo and even gave her another officer and a few men of some caliber. Like a hot roller at a craps table the Navy let 'er ride.

Until the war ended she went and came back, went and came back, like a particularly ugly and dumb bitch abandoned in the woods. Her crew called her the *Underway* and the Navy became first embarrassed and then irritated by her longevity.

By the time they were free to scrap her, she had a tradition and champions, hundreds of officers and men who had served aboard her and counted those months as the worst of their lives, yet with a perversity of human nature better left unexamined they did not want to see her dismantled.

She was like so many Norfolk bargirls: too old and ugly to love, but too many laughs to junk.

And so she stayed in commission, doing those things the Alligator Navy—amphibious fleet—does in peacetime, which are essentially the same things it does during war: onloading and offloading troops and equipment. The only difference is that no one fires at them during peacetime, with the exception of an occasional native with a .22 who can't bring himself to cheer the sight of American Marines swarming onto what he foolishly believes to be his home.

The *Begonia* delivered the goods to Korea when she was called upon, but by the time Vietnam rolled around things had changed and she was not invited into the fray. Either the Pacific Fleet had all it needed or the *Begonia* was no longer to be trusted or . . . whatever. Only fools or those unfortunates who spend endless hours spit-polishing their boots in the brig try to justify the ways of the Navy to man.

Her existence continues as it has and as it will. She leaves Norfolk. Next day she picks up the Marines at Morehead City, North Carolina. She berths them, like the roaches, far from the light of day, in her lowest decks. The crew has an hour or so to touch land one more time and pick up a supply of skin books and cellophane-wrapped sandwiches at the little gedonk at the end of the pier. Then it's off to Vieques to offload the troops and shoot up the island. Before four months have passed and they are back in Norfolk, the sailors will be given a few days to taste the several pleasures of San Juan, not the least of which is fried chicken good enough to make Kentucky Colonel look like Silly Putty.

She drops off the Marines in North Carolina, where they belong, and returns to Norfolk, where no one belongs. The crew is given rolling seventy-two-hour passes so that they can take their package of five duty-free fifths home or to a hotel room. Two or three months later she goes back to Morehead City, but this time heads across the long water to the Mediterranean, where the Marines will shoot up Sardinia in earnest, and in jest tear up Palma de Mallorca, where folks are beginning to get testy about it.

Barring contingencies, she returns to Norfolk after seven months have passed. But there is always a contingency, usually a Soviet submarine, a snake in the garden to the U.S. Navy. Ship's crew is often frightened by the fiery glow that comes into the old man's eyes when he's tracking down a Soviet sub, holding the ears of the sonar receiver like a Frenchman holding his lover.

This cruise, the contingency came early and all that was lost was a liberty stop at Palermo, a port not internationally known for its good liberty. During the time that was to have been liberty, the Soviet sub surfaced near the *Begonia* to take pictures of it. The *Begonia's* photographer's mate second class carried his equipment to the bridge and elbowed his way through the throng of officers and men with their Instamatics in order to set up and snap innumerable pictures of the sub. When both sides had taken more than enough pictures to paper the bulkheads of their captains' staterooms, and the sub still would not submerge, the crew was called to general quarters to keep a wary eye on her for eight hours until she finally disappeared to the depths.

But all that is behind them now.

The sailor walks into the head with his damp towel around his neck and says, "Mornin', Ditty Bag."

John Baggs is hardly visible because he is at the end of the row of washbasins sitting naked in his pan of hot water, his back against the bulkhead. Two asses of men bent over basins are one after the other in front of his face. He cranes his neck to return the greeting. Water sloshes over the sides of his pan as the ship rolls. He sits like a mad meditator, his hairy arms around his hairless legs. (One of the properties of Navy-issue blue wool trousers is that they wear away hair.)

Hair is not the only thing you lose in the Navy. Spend enough time there and you lose your name. John Baggs, for instance, became Fuckin' Aye John Ditty Bag.

A ditty bag is a bleached muslin bag with a drawstring. You are given one in boot camp and you stencil your name and serial number across the side of it and you tie it in a specified way to the rail at the end of your bunk. It is the size of a five-pound flour sack but into it you stuff ten pounds of laundry, like a bliffy, putting off the time you have to scrub your linens in a bucket of water. If you stuff your ditty bag too full the company commander will find you out and tear your bag off your rack, scatter your laundry on the deck, and line up the company to march over it for an hour or so. If afterward you fail to say, "Thank you, sir," you might get his leather gloves across your face and an hour of pushing the piece in the drying room, where it is always 120 degrees. This has happened to Baggs more than once. More than twice. He looks in every port for his old company commander, Lynn Forshay. He is going to kill him, he says, for so many mental reasons.

After boot camp a sailor has no more use for his ditty bag, but most sailors keep it for sentimental reasons.

No one knows who first got carried away saying "Fuckin' aye" and wound up with the melodious invective "Fuckin' aye John Ditty Bag," but since then any number of sailors have gilded the lily and produced things like, "Fuckin' well told aye John Ditty Bag I be go to hell on a forklift!"

Baggs didn't stand a chance in the Navy, what with lucky bags and douche bags and scum bags, but out of graciousness earned by his lighthearted and irresponsible nature, his shipmates called him Fuckin' Aye John Ditty Bag, and any diminutive thereof.

The sailor with the damp towel, which he now suspects may be serving double duty, wins a basin next to Baggs. He holds his douche bag between his legs as he washes.

"So how's the water in your whatchacallit bath?"

"Sitz bath," says Baggs.

"Yeah, sitz bath. Why they call it sitz?"

"You never heard of Seaman Sitz?"

"What division's he in?"

"Seaman Sitz is no longer among the living, but who can

forget that night of gallantry when Seaman Sitz plugged up the
leaking boiler with his own ass?"

"So when are they gonna amputate, Ditty?"

"You've got the mark of the savage on you, lad."

2

HE'S SOAKED his ass in scalding water. He swings through the mess decks, where he wants no chow but fills his huge mug with coffee and continues on his way to the ship's office. He bounces from bulkhead to bulkhead, losing half the coffee and burning his fingers to match his behind.

The ship's office is amidships, so that if the *Begonia* takes a direct hit or has a collision no important papers or records will be lost to the deep six through a gaping hole in the ship's shell. There is no view of the water from amidships, and the stomach abhors the arrangement when the seas are rough, as now.

Baggs holds his coffee mug on his desk with both hands. With his heel he pulls his chair toward him and sits tenderly on a Mae West. The ship rolls so far over that he has to hold down the typewriter. His ass is murdering him.

When he first noticed it was painful to sit down, he tried to ignore the condition. When it did not go away, he went below to sick bay, where he expected no more than the customary envelope of APCs (All-Purpose Capsules), the GI cure for everything.

Sick bay.

The doctor is out, naturally, but Baggs bends over and spreads his cheeks for the corpsman, who says, "Marry me and I'll ship over."

"C'mon, doc, I'm hurting."

"Well, I'll tell you what I think it is, if you promise not to get hysterical."

10

Baggs will not promise.

"I think it's a pilonidal cyst," says the corpsman.

"A what?"

"A pilonidal cyst right there where the spine says Hi to the asshole. I can see the red little bastard."

"So what do we do about it?"

Baggs expects a lancing but hopes that salve or heat or the APCs will take care of it.

"This sort of thing ain't a pimple, Ditty."

"The knife, huh, doc?"

"The *knife*," says the corpsman with a whittler's smile.

"Then let's do it and get it over with. This thing is giving me a pain in the ass."

"Keep up your sense of humor; you'll need it."

"What the heck?"

"You think I can give it a slice with the knife and you're home free. Well, I got tragic news for you. Stick your dog tags between your teeth."

"C'mon, doc, cut the crap. What do we do for it?"

"You can start by getting on the good side of Jesus."

"Watch your mouth," says Baggs. "When's the real doctor going to be in?"

"He's all tied up with circumcisions. We're gonna be under way for another ten days before the next liberty, so all the guys are gettin' circumcised. He's done ten in the past two days, and now he's promotin' it, tellin' the crew that it's more fun screwin' if you're circumcised. He tells the uglies that girls get turned off by uncircumcised peters, so they're all signing up. He's the busiest man aboard. He's savin' up all the foreskins; gonna make himself a wallet."

"You sure know how to enjoy yourself, doc."

"It'll be terrific. When he rubs it, it'll turn into a suitcase."

It is the latest standing joke in sick bay. The corpsman laughs

11

until his eyes water. Baggs stands by until he is able to speak again.

"But the doctor can't take care of you anyway, Ditty."

"Why not?"

"A pilonidal cyst ain't an ingrown toenail. They gotta cut half your ass away."

"Oh, cut the crap."

"I ain't kidding you. It's thirty days in the hospital."

"Cut it out."

"I mean it."

Baggs can see that he does.

"Thirty days?"

"Not a day less. Listen, I know about these things, Ditty. I went to corpsman school."

Prior to that he went to reform school.

"What causes it? Can it be malignant?" asks Baggs.

"It hasn't happened yet, Ditty, but knowing you . . . You ever see one cut open?"

"Of course not. I never heard of one till now."

"You're in for a treat. Ask them to show you what comes out of it."

"What?"

"Blood and water."

"Yeah?"

"And bone."

"Bone?" asks Baggs. "Right there at the asshole?"

"In the business we call it the postanal dimple. Cute, huh? There's also hair in it."

"Hair, too?"

"Ditty, I hate to break this to you, but it's the twin you never had."

A devilish grin is making its way across the corpsman's face.

"Twin?"

"Ditty, that's your brother in that cyst!"

The corpsman laughs himself to his knees.

"Why does everything happen to me?" wonders Baggs.

"You!" shoots back the corpsman, trying to get to his feet. "You! Think of your poor boyfriend, you selfish pig. This is a long cruise."

When Baggs does get to see the real doctor, he bends over to display his affliction. The doctor flashes his light up Baggs' backside and says, "You got it, lad. Pilonidal cyst. The *knife.*"

He says it as an ordained Baggs would have said, *"The Body of Christ. . . ."*

The doctor explains that one theory holds that the cyst is a twin that never took hold, finally appearing in the patient's twenties as a lump of old hair, bone, and blood at the doorway to the anus.

"Do you think you can last to the end of the cruise?" asks the doctor.

"Then what?"

"Thirty days in the hospital at Portsmouth."

"Thirty days? That means I'd be transferred off the *Begonia.*"

"Right."

Behind every cloud . . .

"If I have to, I have to," says a heroic Baggs, hiding his mixed emotions.

"That's the stuff," says the doctor. "In the meantime, sitz baths every four hours, hot as you can stand it. Corpsman, give him a pan."

The doctor is about to turn to other matters, when he says, "I didn't notice: you circumcised?"

Baggs is first in the office, as usual. He has never been able to escape his middle-class inclination to do his job as well as he can. He insists that this does not in itself make him a respectable and responsible person. It is just his nature. Given a job to do, he finds it easier and more pleasant to do it well than to avoid doing it or to do it beneath his capacity so that no one will ever order him to do it again. This has always put him out of step with his shipmates.

No work will be done in ship's office today anyway. Baggs hears the bosun's pipe, followed by the announcement, "Now, prepare for heavy seas. Prepare for heavy seas."

Baggs makes a corner of two heavy manuals for his coffee mug, and he puts the typewriters on the deck. He battens down with elastic bands the op orders, regs, and manuals that are out of file. He opens his desk drawer and checks his homemade "Lost at Sea Survival Kit." In a plastic sack: a small flashlight, fishing line and hooks, can opener, APCs, two cans of tuna fish, small jar of antipasto, rye crisps, small jar of black caviar, pocket knife, folding fork, and a paperback copy of the *Guinness Book of World Records*.

He ties the sack at its end and checks the large safety pin which will attach the sack to his Mae West. He puts the survival kit back into the drawer and withdraws a box of Saltines.

He lies down on the ship's office worktable, hooking his heels at two corners and his elbow at another corner to keep him in place. With his free hand he nibbles Saltines. His mind speaks soothingly to his stomach.

The third class comes in, a tough, wiry kid from Detroit named Wertz, who has a hiding place somewhere where he draws seascapes with a set of colored pencils. Only one person knows where it is, a messboy who stumbled upon it one early evening and got a violet pencil in the arm for his discovery. The corpsman told him he would die of blood poisoning, but he didn't.

Wertz carries his own box of Saltines. His acne is turning from purple to green. He looks at Baggs with disgust.

14

"Your education doin' you any good now, lying there about to chuck your cookies?"

Wertz hates Baggs for his wasted education. He wears a short-timer's chain from his belt, a dangling length of chain with ten links. As each month passes he cuts away another link. He's been wearing it for eight months.

He sits at his desk and puts his head in his arms. First the rear legs of his chair rise slightly and then the front legs rise, as the ship rolls.

"Jesus, for the streets . . ." laments Wertz.

"Watch your mouth," says Baggs.

Fisher arrives with papers in his hand. His color is no better than Wertz's. He was the duty yeoman last night and evidently is in the middle of something. Fisher is an owlish seaman from Dubuque who tries his best to please. Whenever the old man calls down for a NAVPERS 16045 dated 2–8–70, Fisher searches diligently. When the captain calls twenty minutes later wondering where in the hell it is, Fisher says, "Sir, would you settle for a NAVOPS 2172 dated 6–3–70?"

Sometimes the old man screams.

Fisher gets on the intercom to the bridge.

"Bridge, ship's office. The captain up there?"

"Puking over the port side," comes the answer from the watch.

"How about the XO?" asks Fisher.

"Puking over starboard."

Fisher runs out to puke over the fantail.

Seaman Brown comes into the office, eating dry cereal from the box. In every division there is at least one man who never gets seasick, and he always says to the others, "Let's go down to the mess decks and get us a plate of greasy pork chops and sauerkraut with gravery."

In this division it is Brown.

15

Wertz throws the confidential mail log at him, but in his weakened condition the log falls short of Brown's feet.

When Brown first reported aboard the *Begonia,* he spoke to no one and answered all questions in monosyllables. He sat in the office in his dress blues for forty-eight hours, next to his seabag, as though waiting for the bus to take him away from all of this. When they slid a typewriter and roughs in front of him, he typed.

Finally he announced that, proportionate to height, weight, and shoe size, he had the world's largest penis.

Naturally he was challenged to prove it.

He drew out the thing and said, "This is its 'at rest' size."

The yeomen gathered around and inspected it, and the consensus was that it was probably a bit on the small side. Middle-average, to stretch it a bit.

Brown called them ignoramuses.

He sits at his desk and eats cereal like Crackerjacks.

Fisher comes back, white as a cumulus, and Brown says, "Got a greasy old knackwurst samwich for you, with hot sauerkraut."

Fisher races away again, almost knocking over Chief Hayes, who comes in and shouts, "Let's *hit* it!"

He expects them to work.

"Liberty tonight for all hands," he says, "but there's no boats to the landing."

The chief is not feeling too well either and must amuse himself to keep his mind away from his stomach.

"Hey, Baggs, I saw Forshay down in ship's store," he says.

"I saw him in the head," says Wertz.

"I saw him in my douche bag," says Brown.

"I saw him in my dreams," answers Baggs.

Forshay is Baggs' old company commander, the one he hopes to murder someday. Lynn Forshay, signalman first class:

16

Caucasian, blond hair, gray eyes, 1″ scar on right side of upper lip. Ht: 5′6″ Wt: 128 lbs. Sadistic, a result of overcompensation for a feminine name.

In blues, peacoats, and watch caps, Baggs and more than a dozen others were herded by Forshay into the drying room, 120 degrees, where the order was given, "Ready, be*gin*."

They began pushing their pieces. Their pieces are their useless rifles, and they pushed them first out front, then back, then above, then to the side, then back, to above, to the front, back, above, back, to the side, on and on and on and on.

There was not room enough for this martial ballet in the drying room and that fact instilled a savagery in each of them. They became unwilling contestants in a demolition derby. Knock out your friend before he knocks out you.

With his first thrust Baggs took his mate for two good teeth.

Baggs lowered his piece, leaned into the nearest butt, and went down.

He awoke in his own steamy blood, among the first tier of moaning bodies on what could have been the hellboat.

Now Baggs lusts for the destruction of Lynn Forshay.

"I'm in the Navy, he's in the Navy," says Baggs to his shipmates. "I'll run into him."

He groans for his stomach; he groans for his ass.

He keeps in his locker a dog-eared copy of the Bible.

3

VENGEANCE IS MINE, sayeth the Lord, and He minces no words on the subject.

The problem, Baggs believes, is that He seems not to deliver on the promise.

If He did, Forshay would be naked in the cold and snow, but who in modern civilization finds himself naked in cold and snow?

Baggs.

Nine out of ten fire drills occurred when Baggs was in the shower. The laws of probability make coincidence impossible. Deliberate.

You are allowed only your towel. It is forbidden to destroy the beautiful balance of a properly dressed bunk by tearing away the blanket. So it is naked and wet into subzero Great Lakes weather until the all clear is sounded. (Irrelevant that the barracks are fireproof; it is the drill itself that matters.) All that saved those men betrayed in the shower was that their dressed mates were allowed to encircle the naked ones, to press them to keep them from freezing. Baggs owed his life to them, many times over, and during a fire drill he often contemplated how much more he had in common with a Soviet seaman recruit than with his own American superiors.

Their final liberty of the cruise is in Barcelona.

Baggs starts with the others in his division, each with his own concept of what constitutes good liberty.

Chief Hayes takes the duty because he saves all his money for his family back in South Carolina. For this he is ridiculed roundly. Fisher combs the city with three or four Japanese cameras hanging from his neck, in search of old Spanish men in berets sweeping the streets. No one sweeps the streets in Dubuque. Wertz is a gourmet and switchblade fancier. He buys unidentified frying objects from curbside cooks who squat in front of squares of hot sheet metal, turning their delicacies in the sputtering grease. He searches in dark stalls for new and exciting weapons and illegally sneaks them aboard ship in his socks. He has a scar that only Hollywood could reproduce where one popped open accidentally and tore into his ankle. Seaman Brown concentrates solely on the girls and averages three assignations per liberty. It is the girls (and who should know better?) who have informed him that he possesses, proportionately speaking, the world's largest penis.

Baggs looks for Forshay.

For him, cameras are puzzles for the idle, switchblades are courage for the cowardly, and girls . . .

(Baggs, during the long train ride back from leave in Paris to his ship in Cannes. He sits in a compartment with a French mother and her two preteen daughters, prim and neat in matching little uniforms. They try out their English on him. Everyone is having a good time. He wants to offer them something to drink, but notices he has been leaking. A wet stain is at his crotch. He excuses himself, holding his AWOL bag in front of him, and goes to the head to change his pants. John Baggs, *this* close to a clerical collar, with an oozing discharge of pus. Back in the compartment they have a fine time again. Soon, however, a stain becomes visible on these trousers as well. He smiles at the French mother and her daughters. They would faint in horror if they knew. He excuses himself again and goes to change into his last pair of trousers. This time he rolls on a prophlyactic, locking the barn well after the horse has been stolen.)

From bar to bar, attraction to attraction.

"Hi. You guys from the *Intrepid,* huh? Listen, do you have a first class or chief signalman aboard named Forshay? Little guy, blond hair, a Richard Widmark type?"

There are many vessels in the U.S. Navy.

The yeomen meet again near liberty's end at a sidewalk café.

"Saw Forshay at the bullfights," says Fisher. "I think I got a good shot of him for you, if you'll pay for the prints."

"I saw him with a pussful of *paella,*" says Wertz. "He called you a pussy."

"I had a *cerveza* with him at a whorehouse," says Brown. "He insulted your mother."

Baggs is so used to it he hardly hears them. They speak for each other's amusement, not his. They order a round of drinks.

A Marine pfc at the next table is harassing Fisher, calling him a fag. Wertz mumbles toughly about slipping the punk a shiv, but like Brown he tries to pretend nothing is amiss. Fisher agrees that he is a fag, but this only infuriates the Marine further.

Baggs, the ranking man present, says, "Back off, trooper."

The Marine is on his feet.

"Back off? Nobody tells me to back off. I don't back off from *no*body."

"Sit down, then," says Baggs.

"I don't sit down for *no*body. You're messing with the wrong dude, fuckface. I just got finished with eight months of killer training."

And eager to try it all out. What good is it otherwise?

Wertz and Brown are spectators. "Hit him with your Yashica, Fisher," cheers Brown. "Pretend he's Forshay, Ditty," yells Wertz.

20

The Marine jumps into his attack position. He tries a karate step-over-rear kick that pulverizes the air two feet in front of Baggs. The accompanying scream is a fine piece of work. The Marine defends himself against blows that are not forthcoming, blocking beautifully. He attacks again and misses again. In benediction, Baggs knocks him cold with a bottle of mineral water.

Wertz tells the punk to learn his lesson or it will be worse next time.

4

THE *BEGONIA* COMES home to Norfolk. The exact time of the tying of the first line to the pier is noted and recorded to determine the winner of the anchor pool. Baggs stands on deck in the cool dusk and watches the motley little band of dependents waiting for the gangplank to be lowered. The wives are laughing and crying and waving their babies' hands. Some of these babies will be seeing their fathers for the first time. Baggs wonders would he like a wife and child waiting for him on the pier. He can make out the captain's family and the XO's family. They stand aloof. They will be the first to board.

He sees other sailors leaning over the rail to wave at their dependents. He feels the usual clutch at his heart because no one is waiting ashore for him. He will not even bother lining up at the pierside telephone. There is no one to call to tell that the cruise is over and the sailor is home from the sea.

Yet this is the better way to be. For him there is no anguish of separation, no melancholia if mail call holds nothing for him, no staying aboard during overseas liberties in order to save a few pennies for the dependents. *Dependents.* A disarming word. No man should have them, least of all a sailor. Be responsible for your watch and inspections, nothing else.

Since he is to be transferred to the Portsmouth Naval Hospital for thirty days' temporary duty (the duty being to bare his ass to the *knife*), he is snookered out of his seventy-two-hour pass and must stay aboard with the duty until the others have had their passes. He does not mind so much, though he grouses like hell just to hold up his end of one of life's rituals. He enjoys the ship at rest with only a skeleton crew. The officers won't be seen for weeks, thank God. There is a casual routine and room to stretch out a bit. The quality of chow picks up. Like churches and schools and most other institutions, a ship is more beautiful devoid of people.

Baggs has an opportunity to consult with the corpsman on the duty medical guard ship. A pilonidal cyst, he confirms.

Baggs hops the carryall to Portsmouth Naval Hospital and bends over for the duty doctor.

"The *knife.*"

When the rolling seventy-twos are over and the furloughs about to begin, Baggs does his own paperwork and transfers himself to the hospital. He wraps his records in a manila envelope, types his orders, and gets them signed. Guarding his precious papers vigilantly, he packs his seabag and waits in ship's office for the carryall.

"You better pray the doctor don't slip and lop off your gonies," says Brown.

"Goddam, Baggs," says the chief, "don't go asking for a burial at sea. We just got back."

"Watch your mouth," says Baggs.

"Do you think they'd let me photograph the operation?" wonders Fisher.

"Bend over, Ditty," says Wertz. "I'll do it cut-rate, satisfaction guaranteed."

Everyone must say something.

"See you in thirty days," says Baggs as he leaves the ship.

He does not know what he is saying. One Baggs is left behind, another about to be born.

5

PILONIDAL CYSTS may be a mystery to Baggs, but on the seventh floor of the hospital there is a separate ward for them. Two separate wards, actually. One for officers and one for men. Actually, there is a ward for men and a series of semiprivate rooms for officers.

The ward is almost at capacity. Baggs looks over the two long rows of beds, occupied by others with his affliction. The two beds closest to the glass-encased nurses' station hold patients just out of surgery, lying on their stomachs, unconsciously consuming bottles of glucose.

Look upon yourself, John Baggs.

He looks at the others and can almost guess their level of rehabilitation. Some lie sleeping on their stomachs, some read on their sides, some write letters sitting up in bed. Others pace the ward like prisoners on exercise, or sit on foam cushions in the glass-encased TV room at the far end of the ward. There is a steady flow of traffic to the head for sitz baths.

All are purged of their twins and mourning the loss.

Baggs puts necessary items into his night table, including his Bible, the complete poems of Edna St. Vincent Millay, and his college physics crammer. He hangs his seabag on a hook in the seabag locker next to the head. He changes into his hospital gown and slips into bed for some sack time.

His neighbor says, "How you doing? I'm Murphy."

"Baggs."

They reach to each other and shake hands.

24

"The doctor'll take a look at you tomorrow and cut you up the next day."

Shudder.

"And it *hurts*, hoss," says Murphy. "Mother, does it ever hurt! Give your heart to Jesus, Baggs, you're gonna leave your ass on that table."

"Watch your mouth."

"I'm tryin' to let you know what to expect. Look at those two. They just had it. They wish they was dead."

"Thing is," says Baggs, "past couple of days it hasn't hurt so much. In fact, it doesn't feel like anything now.

Murphy smiles condescendingly.

"Too late now, hoss," he says.

"Say, did you ever run into a first class or maybe a chief named Forshay?" asks Baggs.

6

IN THE MORNING those patients closest to discharge help the corpsmen to distribute the chow trays. Baggs sits on the edge of his bed eating and trying to avoid the sadistic smile on Murphy's face. Murphy says, "How sweet it is to have it over with and not have to think about the future."

After chow the patients who are able sweep and swab down the deck. At five minutes before seven o'clock a corpsman announces that the doctor is approaching to make his rounds. This causes a flurry of activity and everyone, with the exception of the two at the end of the ward, gets out of bed and straightens up his night table and stands waiting at the side of the bed.

The doctor can be seen striding toward the ward, his white gown trailing behind him, an entourage joining him as he sweeps forward.

He pauses at the outset and winces. Baggs imagines that peering into thirty assholes is not the best of all possible ways to begin every day.

But the doctor takes the plunge and is under way.

The men lift their gowns in turn and bend over their beds, supporting themselves on their elbows, like post-virgins ready for a new kind of love they have not yet learned to enjoy.

The doctor, between professional mumbles to his scribes regarding progress, condition, and medication, keeps up a running line of chatter, to each man, to all men. He does not end with one and begin with another, but treats it all of a piece, like running across a brook, rock to rock to rock to dry land.

26

"So," he says, "so you're still not over the ordeal of the pilonidal. You think, It's out, it should be over. Toughen up. Quit bitching and count yourself lucky. Do you have any idea of how many cysts the human body is heir to?"

"No, sir," says the patient, but in fact he does. He's compared his tally with the count of others on the ward and they've come up with an approximate figure of 120.

"If you had 'em all at once, son, you wouldn't be a pretty picture. How'd you like a chocolate cyst? Sounds tasty, huh? *Ugh!*" The doctor grasps his own throat. "*Ugh!*" he says again. "I won't tell you why they call it chocolate. You can figure it out for yourself. Double *ugh!* Would you like to have a cyst named after you? Is that the kind of immortality that appeals to you?"

"No, sir," says the next in line.

"Baker made it. Blessig made it. Boyer made it. Poor Gärtner gave his name to a duct and then damned if the duct didn't come up with its own cyst—the gartnerian. Oh, brother, the cyst business. You keeping up the sitz baths, hot as you can stand it? Every *two* hours for you."

He moves to the next man.

"How'd you like a hydatid cyst, son?"

"I wouldn't like that, sir."

"You bet your ass you wouldn't. It's a nightmare cyst. You think you got one but you got a thousand. A regular sorcerer's apprentice of a cyst. Fissural, follicular, adventitious . . ."

He moves on and asks the next man, "Can I sell you a dentigerous cyst today, son?"

"Not today, sir."

"Why not? There's a cyst with some bite in it."

He laughs alone at his private joke.

"You want to know why they call it chocolate? I'll tell you

why. Because it contains dark syrup, resulting from an accumulation of sticky brownish serum. *Ugh! Ugh!*"

Baggs can feel the morning coffee backing up. His knees grow weak.

"And you kids feel sorry for yourselves. Grow the hell up! You ain't seen nothin' yet. Try the lively seminal cyst, the milky chyle cyst, the bloody extravasation-type cyst. You feeling soiled? How'd you like a few soapsuds cysts? That sounds clean and harmless enough? You're crazy! They'll turn your brain into yogurt!"

Baggs notices that the doctor begins to tremble. What's more, Baggs himself begins to tremble.

"And then the thing to do," continues the doctor, jabbing his thumb at the deck, "is to drop to your knees and thank the dear Lord that you're not a woman, because women are open to a bunch of cysts you guys will never see, thank the dear Lord, because they would knock your eyes right out of your head."

"Yes, sir," sing several patients in unison.

Finally, the doctor is at Baggs.

"New man, huh? Well, Baggs, we run a tight ship here. Mind your *p*'s and *q*'s, we'll be pals. Step out of line and I'll have you in a bottle of formaldehyde. I have a nice selection of aneurysmal bone cysts today. Would you like to trade your scrawny pilonidal for one of those?"

"No, sir, I guess I'll just hold pat."

"You're nobody's dummy, right?"

"No, sir."

The doctor casts some light up Baggs' backside. He hums as long as he dares and then falls into total, unprofessional self-betrayal when he says, "Wow!"

Baggs sees Murphy turn around and smile. Murphy draws his forefinger across his throat.

The doctor slaps his own forehead and plops onto a chair.

C-c-c-can-can-can . . . Baggs cannot say the word to himself.

"I've seen pilonidal cysts," says the doctor to no one in particular, "I daresay I've seen as many as any man alive, but this is the week that was."

What the hell does *that* mean? wonders Baggs. Murphy covers his mouth with both hands.

C-c-c-can-can . . . It's *got* to be.

"Corpsman," says the doctor in an incredulous tone, "take this man to the examination room. Shave him. I have to have a closer look-see."

Baggs, knees buckling, is led away by a corpsman. He hears Murphy whistle gratingly through his teeth, like the opening of a vacuum-packed can.

Belly down on a leather-top table. A sliding shelf is placed flat against the top of Baggs' head. The corpsman turns the crank and the table breaks away, falls, and rises in such a way that Baggs' ass is at the highest point, his head is resting on the shelf, and he doesn't know where his legs are. They are at some level between his head and his ass.

Up goes his gown. He feels the razor scraping at his buttocks.

"You see the New York-Philly game last weekend?" asks the corpsman.

"I don't follow sports," says Baggs. *Scrape, scrape, scrape.*

"See any good movies lately?" asks the corpsman.

"I just came back from the Med, haven't even had a liberty ashore yet."

Cut down in his prime, his whole life ahead of him.

Scrape, scrape, scrape.

"Politics," says the corpsman, a born barber. "It's getting so you can't tell one liar from another without a score card."

"You're right, you're right."

"What do you think of all this women's lib horseshit?"

"Please, doc . . ." says Baggs.

"Right. Just trying to be friendly."

He finishes and leaves the room, leaving Baggs with the blood rushing to his palpitating brain.

Finally, the doctor arrives.

"All right, now, Baggs boy, let's have another look at your whatchacallit."

There is a roaring in Baggs' ears.

The doctor spreads the buttocks and looks for the longest time. Always he is humming. He cranks the table to the normal position, and Baggs sits upright, light-headed.

"Who in the hell was the doctor that admitted you?"

"I believe it was you, sir," says Baggs.

"Me? Me?"

"I believe so, sir."

"Then there must be a logical explanation."

"What's wrong with me, sir?"

The Lord giveth and He taketh away, and what was Earth becomes once again Earth.

The doctor tears off a rubber glove. He is irritated.

"Not a damn *thing*," he says.

"But . . . but . . ."

"The only thing I can figure is that you had a hell of a boil. . . . Are you subject to boils?"

"I've had a few, sir."

"Ah, ha. If you had one, you'll have nine. Ask anyone who knows. A boil in the ass and a pilonidal cyst are two different balls of wax." It hits him. "Two *diff*erent . . ." He must laugh at his joke.

The medical profession is not without its native humor, muses Baggs, still a bit dizzy.

"My guess is those sitz baths . . . Have you been taking sitz baths?"

"Every four hours, sir."

"That's *it*. The sitz baths brought the boil to a head and it ran its course. I can see redness and scar tissue there. Did you ever notice a stain on your skivvies?"

"Yes, sir, I did."

"And you don't inhale cigarettes, do you?" he asks, smiling.

This doctor is mad, thinks Baggs.

"Had to be a boil. Gone now," he says.

"I can leave the hospital, then?"

"Just as soon as they process you and do the paperwork, son."

For some reason the doctor shakes Baggs' hand.

Baggs stops to confer at the medical station and then walks back to the ward. The other patients are all waiting at the edges of their beds.

"You're gonna *die,* ain't you?" asks Murphy.

Baggs nods bleakly. "There's no point operating," he says. "I only have about a week."

They were just kidding around! They didn't mean anything! Murphy wants to cut his own throat.

"I told the doc I want to spend my last days with you guys."

(Baggs has learned at the medical station that it takes seven days to process and discharge an in-patient. The minimum stay, whatever the reason, must be seven days.)

At night Murphy sobs in his bed for his fallen comrade and his own despicable cruelty.

7

IT IS NOT a bad deal. Given seven days' leave he would go to New York and drink, gamble, and fornicate with New York women, returning to the ship an exhausted and wasted man. This way he will get seven days' bed rest and then he will be *ready* for New York.

But in the morning he is sent to the master-at-arms to be given some work to do until his discharge. Murphy and the others sulk and gripe about the inhumanity of putting a dying man to work. They talk about organizing some sort of protest, but Baggs tells them he would rather work.

Truth is, he would rather not work. And as it turns out, he does not have to.

The MAA looks at his ward number and stamps his card WARD DUTY, explaining to his assistant, "The guys from this ward have to take baths every four hours; you can't take 'em away from the ward."

A lucky break, but the irony is that he must continue the sitz baths.

He whispers to the lieutenant (jg) nurse, "There's nothing wrong with me, ma'am. I'm just waiting for the paperwork."

"Here's your chart. Read it for yourself."

"A mistake, obviously. Why should I have to take sitz baths when I don't have one of those cysts?"

"This ward is a ship and the doctor is its captain," says the nurse.

32

No other explanation is necessary. Baggs takes sitz baths every four hours.

In between baths, he plays Monopoly. He suspects they are letting him win. He reads the Bible, he reads his poetry, he crams for physics exams he will never take. Like the other ambulatories he is allowed to eat evening chow down below in the mess hall, where the chow is hot and plentiful. It is the best chow Baggs has had in the Navy.

He takes a swab in the morning and helps clean the deck. That is what is meant by WARD DUTY. Even considering the sitz baths, this is the best duty he's ever pulled. He puts a fine edge on his cribbage game.

The doctor makes his rounds and continues his routine as though another day has not passed. When he gets to Baggs he looks up his backside and says, "What would you say to a nice globulomaxillary cyst, son?"

"I'd say, 'Walk on by,' sir."

"Don't even tip your hat," says the doctor.

He examines Baggs again the next morning.

Every morning he examines Baggs.

As new patients are admitted Murphy points out the terminal case to them. He reminds them it could happen to them too.

Seven days pass. On the eighth morning Baggs whispers to the doctor, "Sir, shouldn't I be discharged?"

"Patience, son, patience. There are fellows here much longer than you."

He examines Baggs the following morning.

Ten days. Twelve days. Finally Baggs makes demands upon the nurse and corpsmen, who try to stay within their glass-encased shell. Something is wrong, they agree darkly over their coffee mugs. It has always been like clockwork. Seven days exactly to discharge a patient back to duty. A messenger is dispatched to get to the bottom of this.

Baggs sits on his bed and nibbles his fingernails. There will come unto him a prophet of gloom and he shall be clothed in Navy blue.

Murphy thinks he understands Baggs' uneasiness. He knows that Baggs is already living on borrowed time. He pats Baggs on the knee and says, "Hang in there, big fella."

It is more than two hours before the messenger returns to the medical station. Baggs can see them in their consternation, each trying to get the other to do something no one wants to do. The ranking nurse raises her hand and the others fall silent and still. (In jungle combat, so it's said, many officers would not wear the insignia of rank. The Japanese snipers would have to wait in their trees for someone to raise his hand, just so, and this one would be shot. Baggs has the instincts of a jungle sniper.) She points at the messenger. The detail is his, he is the lowest rank among them, a seaman-deuce-corpsman-striker, only a few grains of sand higher than whale shit.

He grumbles and shuffles toward Baggs, looking everywhere except at Baggs. Baggs feels himself go down like a rock in water.

The messenger says, as he approaches him, "Look, Baggs, it didn't happen on my watch."

The Navy theme song.

"Yes?"

"Somebody down below in the offices . . ."

"Yes?"

"Well, what they did is lose all your records."

Baggs can only close his eyes and wonder what sin it was that now consigns him to limbo.

8

THE AVERAGE CIVILIAN believes a boy joins the Navy because he wants to learn electronics, or he wants to travel, or he wants to return to his source. More likely he joins because it's that or the Army and he doesn't want to have to defecate in his helmet and later cook in it, or a judge tells him to join or go to jail, or he wants to slip off the panties of numerous Spanish whores. Or maybe he really *does* want to learn electronics.

In any case, in most lives some small forgotten symbol foreshadowed the eventual enlistment in the Navy. A little gob outfit with a whistle around the neck at age two, a bathtub fleet of men-of-war, a pubescent crush on the swaggering swabby home on furlough and flashing the red fire-belching dragons sewn into his jumper's lining and the blue-black memento of a nautical rite needled into his forearm.

John Baggs, however, joined because at the moment of greatest panic in the face of self-knowledge he wanted to do a thing most irresponsible, and he was philosophically opposed to terminating his life. Instead he joined the Navy, with full intentions to rape, plunder, pillage. He did, in fact, achieve a state of irresponsible grace, and he reenlisted because he was afraid of losing it on the outside. That, and his failure to find Forshay, his old company commander. He was well on his way to becoming a twenty-year man.

He did not plan it that way; very few sailors do. Even the career chief petty officers all have the same story: they came in during the war (one or another) and made rate so rapidly they could not afford to leave the Navy when the war ended.

Most of the peacetime lifers tried to leave the Navy after their first hitch, abusing the poor bastards who still had a couple of years to go. But once outside, they were stripped naked of free medical and dental care, of PX, club, and commissary privileges, of the security of a controlled environment. They had to function alone in an adult society, for which they had received no training in the Navy. Within ninety days, after which one loses his rate at time of discharge, they were scratching like little rats at the recruiter's door.

The Navy will woo you with sugar plums like bonuses and choice duty to get you on the dotted line for that first reenlistment. After that the Navy can ignore you, because if it's had you for six years it has you for life, regardless of who or what you were.

John Baggs, for example, was educated, a semester away from a BS. It was a secret he tried to keep, unsuccessfully, because an educated enlisted man draws three separate reactions in the Navy: distrust from the officers, who believe he might be smarter than they; wonder and awe from the illiterates, who cannot fill out a chit without aid; cruelty from those a chevron above, who know they will never have another opportunity to be superior to a college man.

Baggs was awarded a full scholarship from the Lutheran Church, the Annual Martin Luther Scholarship, for an outstanding high school graduate who desires to enter the ministry.

A pre-theological student can major in anything as an undergraduate, though most are encouraged to major in philosophy, psychology, sociology, the liberal arts. John Baggs chose physics, which called for some tricky explanations to the synod.

His true desire was to get a nifty job with Eastman Kodak.

36

If the Lutherans demanded, he would repay their scholarship out of his tremendous earnings.

What he did not anticipate was the tradition of having the M.L. recipient take the local pulpit one Sunday during his senior year, as student spiritual leader.

Never having imagined he would someday actually have to preach a sermon, Baggs was tasting old food by the time the regular pastor helped him don his black robe. The pastor shook his hand with both hands and walked beside him to the altar singing "A mighty fortress is our God. . . ."

Baggs had agonized a full week over a hypocritical sermon chastising those who take the Lord's name in vain. It was the only topic, apart from the laws of physics, in which he felt some expertise.

"Why is it," he asked his flock, leaning over the pulpit toward them, "that when we hit our thumbs with our hammers, we never cry out in pain and anger, *George Washington!* or *Albert Einstein!* or *Florence Nightingale!* No, we always spit out the dearest name of them all, the name of the Pure One who died for our sins. Why is it," he asked, leaning precariously closer, "that in fury and frustration we never cry out, *Marlon Brando! Lyndon Johnson! Ishka Bibble!* but instead vent our unholy spleens with the holiest of appellations? And when we are surprised and stunned by the rapid turn of events in an uncertain world, do we express our shock by crying, *Kukla, Fran, and Ollie . . .* or *Peter, Paul, and Mary . . .* or *Manny, Moe, and Jack?* Oh, no, it is always *Jesus, Mary, 'n' Joseph!*"

Baggs saw women dab their eyes with hankies, he saw his father and the other men jut out their jaws with pride of him, he saw little boys squirm guiltily as he ran through the catalogue of their sins of blasphemy and profanity.

And the hell of it was, he loved it. He loved toying with all those guilt-ridden souls. What if his subject had been sex? he

wondered. What if he had suggested the theological consequences of getting an erection in the Lord's house for the win-
some blonde three pews in front? There was no end to the power
of a hypocrite in the midst of the Protestant ethic. As he shook
the hands of the departing congregation at the exit of the
church, he could see in their faces the need already to put their
souls into his safekeeping.

He was a boy who took himself seriously, however, and he
wondered if on this day he heard the call that cannot go unan-
swered. Can one ever be sure, really, that one is a hypocrite?
The Lord works in strange ways His miracles to perform.

His mother embraced him and cried openly against his neck.
His father blinked back his own tears and almost broke Baggs'
hand as he shook it. The neighbor's kid, who several times in
the past had sniped him with rocks, now approached him in
awe, quaking with fear and respect.

Was his purpose in life revealed to him this day? Was he to
go forward and spread the Word?

He hoped not.

There were still too many sins beyond his power to abandon.

But the experience had so undone him, that giddy feeling of
having 251 people (the official count that day) in his phony
grasp, that he felt irresistibly drawn to that exalted pulpit. He
would become a minister unless he could do something drastic
to prevent it.

What he did was drop out of school and join the Navy, a
more drastic move than imagined. It caused a total estrange-
ment from family, church, and community, all of whom felt
bilked in the most mean manner. His family moved and did not
give him a forwarding address.

The sermon he preached that Sunday affected more than his
memory. He was never able to practice profanity again without
a devastating sense of guilt and betrayal. It made being a sailor

just that much more difficult. He could not swear, and yet he wanted to swear with the best of them. His swear phrases were all his own: "You dilty plick! You mollywopper! You lump! Go to seed!"

His most brutal thrust of profanity was reserved for the very lowest elements of mankind.

"Eggsucker!"

He never said it unless he meant business.

When he left boot camp for the Real Navy, he wanted duty on the deck force, the dread of all seamen deuces, a Siberia for mental incompetents and those with powerful enemies. He wanted to strike for a bosun's rating, break a Marine's jaw, drink a house painter to the floor, and kiss himself a pretty gal.

But the Navy discovered he could type and his spelling ability was in the ninety-ninth percentile, far above the most literate of commanding officers.

They made a yeoman out of him.

Titless Waves, they called them.

9

BAGGS WITHOUT RECORDS becomes in effect a nonperson locked into his present status and duty station until they either find his records or duplicate them, which can conceivably take until the end of time. He cannot be transferred, he cannot be promoted, he cannot be paid. There is a whole range of things he cannot do.

He *can* remain a hospital patient for the rest of his days.

Murphy and the other guys are as sore as cysts that they have squandered their sympathy on a fraud who is not going to die, and yet in a way is already dead. They abuse him and ridicule him and laugh at his predicament.

Baggs sees Murphy discharged, he sees them all discharged and new ones admitted to take their places, and he sees *them* discharged. When he is pointed out to new patients, they regard him with genuine but distant sympathy. Could it happen to *them?*

Every morning Baggs asks the doctor, "Have they found my records yet?"

And every morning the doctor examines him and like a peddler with a cart offers him one of his wide selection of ghastly cysts.

Routinely, they make him continue to take the sitz baths, but one day he has enough of it. Thereafter, every four hours he sits in his clothes in a dry pan in the head and has a smoke. He is caught at it again and again, but each time the corpsman or nurse pretends not to see him. It is easy to pretend he does not exist. He has no records.

Baggs walks the hospital like a sleepwalker, stopping assorted brass in the corridors, pleading to be plucked out of limbo.

All agree it is grossly unfair that Baggs should find himself in such a situation. Some shake their heads in frustration, some sigh sadly. All admit there is not a thing to be done about it but wait for the records to be duplicated from microfilm, if there really is microfilm, as they say. If there is microfilm, no one seems to know where it is. Some say FBI, others say CIA, Pentagon, NAVPERS. . . .

They are moved at least to grant him liberty, but it is Cinderella liberty: he must be back on the ward every night by midnight.

"Why?"

"Because."

"Because why?"

"Because."

Like conversation with a four-year-old.

So for a time he checks out after every evening chow, walks downtown to look for Forshay (some things remain constant), and by midnight returns drunk to the hospital, where he has turned into something of a character. Staff members smile at him indulgently as he staggers through their corridors. He checks in, finds his bed in the dark, and sleeps the sleep of the nonperson, which is a nonsleep.

Soon he is out of money and must spend his evenings playing Monopoly or cribbage.

10

BAGGS HAS NOT forgotten Forshay, but his vengeance has only half a heart. The loss of his records has weakened him generally and he takes long afternoon naps. One morning he tries to do push-ups next to his bed and he collapses after only five. Baggs, who could snap off a hundred of them in boot camp, Forshay's boot at his head. *Die, Forshay!* The cry shrinks inward.

He becomes listless and vague and agreeable to everything. He says, "Thank you," to insults and compliments alike.

He wakes one night and Forshay is at his bedside, gently shaking his shoulder and cooing, "Ditty Bag, Ditty Bag, guess what? Guess what?"

Baggs knows what. He's been averaging two and a half hours sleep a night because of what.

"What, sir, Mr. Forshay?"

"It's snowing, Ditty. Flakes like half dollars."

Baggs on the sidewalk in front of the MAA's office, with foxtail and dustpan, sweeping up the snow as it lands. He is responsible for the three squares of walkway immediately adjacent to the office. Forshay, the MAA, and his messenger are at the window, drinking hot coffee and laughing at him.

Baggs goes to the office door and sounds off: "*Sir,* Baggs, seaman recruit, 684–21–04, requesting permission to wear foul weather gear, *sir.*"

Baggs can see the foul weather coats hanging on a rack. They are heavy, fur-lined canvas coats and can keep out the cold that is numbing him to the bones.

42

"Well, Baggs," says the MAA, "let's have a look at the temp."

The MAA steps outside and looks at his thermometer.

"Why, lad, you're wasting my time. Look here, it's all of thirty degrees. It's goddam balmy out here. You know damn well that regs say the temp gotta be below thirty for me to issue foul weather gear. When that temp drops to twenty-nine, you come see me, not before. Now get on that snow, lad. It's gettin' ahead of you."

Every time Baggs pauses and looks toward the thermometer, the MAA's hand snakes out of the office and his thumb presses over the bulb of mercury.

In three hours the snow stops and Baggs finally can straighten his aching back. He has kept ahead of it. There is no snow on his three squares.

Forshay pokes his head out of the office and says, "MAA decided he likes it better with the snow on it. Shovel that snow back on the sidewalk."

When Baggs returns from morning chow, he finds the MAA has changed his mind and he must once again remove the snow.

Baggs gets out of bed and goes to the nurses' station looking for a foxtail and dustpan to sweep up the drifting snow. He is led back to bed and given a shot of something.

There is some talk about admitting him to the psycho ward, and a psychiatrist interviews him. Baggs tells him about his single sermon, his experiences with Forshay, his loss of records.

This man has valid reasons for behaving oddly, concludes the psychiatrist, but a stretch in the psycho ward wouldn't hurt him.

They ask Baggs, "Would you like to visit our nut ward?"

"That would be nice," says Baggs. "Thank you."

Baggs is obliged to thank everyone. He has no sustenance of his own.

They do not move Baggs to the nut ward, however, because they cannot move him anywhere. He has no records.

So from one point of view it is better to be lost in pilonidal cysts and go crazy than to be lost in the psycho ward and develop a pilonidal cyst.

11

EVERYONE IS sympathetic to Baggs. When he approaches a man on the ward and says casually, "Hey, hoss, you got a dime?" he always gets the dime. He acts as though it is for a telephone call, an evening paper, a parking meter. At the end of a few days he has raised enough to go downtown and drink himself silly with Old Sly Fox.

Those in charge decide to extend his liberty privileges. They feel sorry for him. On Saturdays and Sundays he may leave the ward at noon and he does not have to return until midnight. If he wants to eat, however, he must come back at five for chow.

He divides his time among the free attractions of the Tidewater area: the shipyard, the library, the bus station, the streets. Sailor places.

For my days are consumed like smoke . . . "Psalm of the Afflicted."

He wears his watchband over his plastic hospital ID bracelet and pretends he is a civilian. In this capacity he sits alone for an hour in an empty church and listens to excerpts from the phony sermons he would have delivered if he had gone through with it. There would have been a cozy parsonage adjoining and in it with him a chubby rural girl who could play the organ. Children would come, one-two-three, and upon them would fall the burden of spiritual parents in a fast and loose society.

Yet this is the better way to be, by yourself, responsible to and for no one, your only duty to be home before midnight. If only there were something to do before midnight. Even Cinderella had a ball.

12

HER NAME IS Maggie Paul. She is not much to look at, except from behind, which is the view Baggs now enjoys. She can do with another fifteen pounds and she is a few years older than he, but he suspects she will cost him nothing, which is to the sailor what "walking the dog" is to a Yo-Yo cuckoo. It is cause enough to wake up your shipmates with the victorious call, "I got it for free!"

He glances at his watch as he follows her up the dusty stairway. He has but an hour.

He looks forward to the pleasure of placing skin upon skin once more. The last time was with a typewriter mechanic in Naples who afterward admitted that she probably preferred women. But even so, it was nice. It is always a pleasure.

They must be quiet, she warns. Her son is asleep on the sofa and her twin girls are asleep in the kitchen.

He follows her through the darkness of the living room. The son sits up.

"It's only me, Doug," whispers Maggie. "Go back to sleep."

Sordid, thinks Baggs, and he says, "Excuse me," to the lad, feeling the kid's contempt jump over the coffee table at him.

It is not unpleasant but not a pleasure either. What does the boy feel with each squeak of the bedsprings? What does he envision when his mother moans? Better to be alone and with records lost than to be that boy on the sofa, lying awake and listening to his mother move in rhythm with the stranger who's mounted her.

To the end of it, the boy is on Baggs' mind.

Maggie has a voice like paper tearing, tempered by a sweet accent not quite southern.

"Are you from this part of the country?" asks Baggs.

"Lord, *no.*"

"Watch your mouth. Where are you from, then?"

"New Orleans. I want to go back there. You got a car?"

"No. Sorry."

"Would you take me home to New Orleans if you did?"

"Probably not . . . unless I was going there anyway."

"Say you would, though."

"Why?"

"Have you ever been there?"

"No."

"If you had, you would say yes."

"You don't need me. Go back to New Orleans if you want to."

"Everything is easy for you," says Maggie Paul. "Try being me."

"How did you wind up here?"

"I was taking my boy Doug to Baltimore. He had something wrong with his eye and this doctor in New Orleans looked at it—he only looked at it, mind—and he said he would have to operate on it. But then I heard of this specialist in Baltimore, at that school there . . ."

"Johns Hopkins."

"That's the place. So I was taking Doug there and we was in Norfolk when some bastard copped my purse, my money, the tickets, everything. Stranded in the jungle. We been here ever since."

"The twins?"

"They were born here."

"What about Doug's eye?"

48

"It seemed to take care of itself."

Squalid, all of it.

"You make a living in that place?" asks Baggs.

"You call this living? The kids get welfare and I get favors from sailors."

"I'd like to give you something."

"Thanks, I could use it."

"Only I don't have anything."

"You got paid but the day before yesterday."

"The rest of the Navy did. I'm in the hospital; things are different for me."

"Nothing vital, I hope. You know, the hospital."

"Maggie, it's a long story. I'm afraid you drew the wrong sailor tonight. I should have told you at the start, but I was too hungry for it."

"Hey, what do you think I am, a lousy hooker? You can just change your point of view right this minute. I like you, what's wrong with that? If you want to give me a favor, I'll take it with thanks. If you don't have anything, well then, God bless you, as they say in the song. Stay the night if you want to, what the hell."

"I would like to, Maggie, but I'm on Cinderella liberty. I got to get moving now, as a matter of fact, or I'm going to be AWOL."

"Come back tomorrow night."

"If I could have stayed the night, what would you have told the kids in the morning?"

"What do you mean?"

Baggs has already said more than is good for him.

"Say, the food at the hospital is terrific. What if I try to bring a bag with me?"

It would be received with thanks. Feeding three kids is never easy and often impossible.

Baggs dresses and leaves Maggie in her bed. He is moved to kiss her and hold her face in his hands. She has been wonderfully good for him. His lethargy has disappeared. He hopes he has been good for her too, but he cannot ask her.

He stops at the sofa. The boy is still awake. Baggs sits on the coffee table and says, "Your mother has a big heart."

The boy says nothing.

Baggs leans toward him and puts a hand on his shoulder.

The boy recoils and says, "Keep your hands to home, you fuckin' faggot!"

He is thirteen. His hair is brown and kinky. Baggs looks closer at the fair, freckled face. It has the broad nose and thick lips of the black man.

Baggs hears the snap and now sees the blade. Another Wertz.

"I'll cut your goddam honky throat," he says.

"Watch your mouth."

A very defensive kid, thinks Baggs. He wonders how many nights the boy has lain here, watching the procession of sailors follow his mother to her bed.

"I want to be your friend," says Baggs.

"I got a friend," says Doug.

The *knife.*

13

THE BOY DOES not make up to him, unlike the twin girls, seven years old, who fawn over Baggs and masticate to fine pulp the apples he has brought them from the hospital.

Soft food for Doug; his teeth are rotten. There is a clinic Maggie has been trying to get him to, but arrangements take forever. Does he keep from smiling because of his rotten teeth?

Thirteen is as lonely as any age, but if you are genetically betwixt and between you are a lonelier thirteen. Doug has opted for his black half, but the blacks have not welcomed him inside, which only redoubles his hatred of whites. There is another half-breed at school but they avoid each other like prima donnas.

He knows the ways of the whites, but then, who doesn't? His knowledge of blacks he gets primarily from the "Flip Wilson Show." Before a mirror he has taught himself how to fight with a switchblade. If ever he has to cut a man up, he believes it will prove who he is.

"You're a bigot," Baggs tells him.

"Honky cop-out."

"No, you're bigoted against blacks. You think they're all knife-fighters."

Doug seethes. He does not have to listen to a lily white tell him about blackness. He tells Baggs so as he slams the door behind him.

The girls, Judy and Trudy, have army surplus cots in the tiny kitchen, but they will not go to bed unless Sailor Baggs carries them there. One hanging from each shoulder, he takes them to the kitchen and tucks them in. They are reflections of each other, but already Baggs can instinctively tell them apart. Each gives him a hug and a kiss.

Such good kids in such bad circumstances.

Will he bring them anything tomorrow?

"I'll try to bring you some cheese. Good protein. Do you like cheese?"

"*Yum*my!"

Do you like cheese? Do they have a choice?

Does Baggs have a choice?

If he had, he would prefer not to get mixed up in this. His own problems do not allow him to take up the cudgel for others' problems. But children cannot be left to despise their youth.

He is inclined to sit with Maggie on her bed and talk about it. Maggie, there are three children to consider. Someday they will be adults, and what then? Will they be kind? You are not free. You can be free any time you choose to be, but if you do not choose to be, then there are three children to consider.

Instead he tells her about how he was lost by the U.S. Navy. The story is longer than it need be, but it is heavier on him than it was. If he were on regular duty, he would do something for them. He might even take them to New Orleans.

"See? I *knew* you would," she says. "New Orleans is like that. I'll stuff you full of pecans and bananas, just see if I don't."

"Instead here I am, a prisoner of peace, not a thing wrong with me, but hospital-bound. There's nothing I can do but wait. I'd ship over for Iceland if they'd let me. I'd do the next four years on water if they'd only give me my records and let me go." Baggs is close to crying. "What do they give me? Cinderella liberty! I can't even spend a whole night with you."

Maggie moves to her knees and holds his arm.

"Johnny," she says, "in one way or the other most of us are on Cinderella liberty."

She puts him on his back and does him a lovely favor, a wifely thing to do. He knows it is just another consolation prize to still another loser who followed her home, but he receives it with long sighs of appreciation. Then, so that there will be no losers, no prizes, he returns the favor, and her own sighs fall upon his that are still in the air.

Later, they kiss, to taste each other and themselves. Baggs clings to her to think of nothing apart from her. It is a moment that becomes an hour.

They are awakened by the slamming of the door. Doug has returned.

"I like that kid," says Baggs. "I wish I could . . . relate to him." It is a word Baggs usually avoids.

"He's moody as hell," says Maggie.

"Why?"

"It's just his way."

"Who was his father?"

"A boy I knew in New Orleans."

Things are only as complicated as we make them.

"And the twins?"

"I had the feeling they had different daddies, but I was told that ain't possibly so."

"There are a lot of people around to tell you what is possible and what isn't."

"Especially if you're a woman."

"Don't listen to them," says Baggs.

"I don't," she says.

"Listen to me."

She puts her ear on it and looks at him along his belly. "I can hear the sea," she says.

14

"Could I ask you a personal question?" she asks, stroking his stomach.

"Sure."

"What's your religion?"

"You really want to know that?" he asks, surprised.

She nods.

"Well, I'm an ex-something or other, I'm afraid," he says.

"I mean, do you have a whole lot of rules and everything you have to follow? Don't do this, don't do that."

"Very few, Maggie. Just a couple of homemaders."

"Reason I ask is, do you like a little punishment once in a while?"

Once Baggs kicked a girl. It was in Old San Juan, and he kicked her to loosen the hold she had on his leg so that he could pull on his pants and make it down the stairs to the street. A contractual dispute. They were in front of the desk clerk at the time and the girl had left behind her a trail of douche Coke. Had he not kicked her he would have had to drag her down the stairs with him and that could have resulted in painful injuries.

Baggs has done several other unsavory things, even with a sailor's pride, but he has never inflicted pain on another for his own pleasure. That will come when he finds Forshay.

"Well, it's kind of fun, you know," says Maggie. "Every once in a while I like to get slapped around first and . . . things. Gives it a little spice. You like getting tied up? We'll try it sometime."

"No, we won't, Maggie. It's abnormal, that stuff."

54

"I've come to find that what's abnormal is what the other fellow digs and you can't stomach."

"I want to be a comfort to you, Maggie, and that's all I ever wanted you to be for me. There are enough hard knocks in the world without me knocking you around, hurting you, and I'm sensitive about my own hurts too."

"You're sweet, you know that?"

"I want to be, because I think you have this . . . this *thing* about you, I don't know, a sense of violence or something, and now you come off telling me you like getting rapped around. I don't want you wanting things like that."

"Violence? Take a look at this."

She lifts up her left arm. The track of the knife runs from the back of her armpit to the curve of her breast.

"I been around," she explains.

"Aw, Maggie . . ."

"One thing about it, you get one or two of these babies and nothing scares you much anymore. Hell, after that a rap on the mouth is a love tap."

Literally.

"Gee, Maggie, is that what they do in New Orleans?"

"A good piece of the time."

"Then why would you want to go back there?"

"Why? Why?" She puts her hands under her head and looks up at the ceiling, bedeviled by his density. "I don't know why," she has to admit. "I only do."

"All that's over now, Maggie. No more raps."

"Sure, Daddy, you're my prince on the white horse."

The prince whoas his steed at the sofa again. With a brilliant flash of insight, Doug calls him an evangelist, or words to that effect.

15

HE BECOMES the nightly visitor, arriving around six with his bag of leftovers. The twins lead him to his chair. Except for a few accouterments he is the country squire. He has no slippers, for instance, but a twin at each foot relieves him of his shoes and he sits comfortably in his socks. Should the twins spy a hole in his sock, they sew it shut for him. Maggie is not allowed near needles because she stabs her fingers in one more manifestation of self-destructiveness.

He has no pipe either, but the girls have learned how to roll Bull Durham, fighting over whose turn it is tonight. They each loop a little finger through the drawstring and pull shut the tobacco pouch like rich kids over a wishbone. He has no newspaper because that's a dime a day, but the news on TV is free, once the set is paid for, which will be never. But what can he care about news of the world anyway? It would be different if he lived in it.

He has no brandy either, but he wouldn't know brandy if he had it. A sip of Old Sly Fox, the official Tidewater beverage.

Maggie has her sips earlier in the day and sometimes is unconscious on the bed by the time Baggs arrives. Then he becomes stew-burner for them, and the twins lean against their folded cots and laugh at the spectacle.

He makes Maggie hot coffee or a gruel. Always to his calling, his first motivation is to moralize, but he knows he is too frail even to pick up the first stone. I will stand by you in your stupor, stand by me in mine. We will call this love.

56

He undresses her and may perhaps slide his hand along her body for that bit of comfort before leaving her to sleep it off.

He plays Fish with Judy and Trudy.

Doug shakes his head, disgusted to be surrounded by losers and incompetents.

"You know what you remind me of, Baggs?"

"I'd love to know."

"A hero."

"Huh?"

"You're the kind of dude who if you heard the neighbor scream murder you'd be in there like supersport."

"Wrong."

"You're the only dude's ever been in this place three times. Goddam hero, that's you."

"Watch your mouth."

"What are you out for, Baggs? To save somebody's soul?" Doug laughs derisively. He makes the sign of the cross and says, "In the name of the Father, and the Son, and the Holy Goose."

"Watch your mouth," says Baggs.

"C'mon, Douglas, we're trying to play a game," says Trudy.

"Clamp your jaw, brat," says Doug. "Losers, all of you. Nobody around here knows how to survive but me. Look out for yourownself, whitey. You're the kind of dude goes around thinking there's some reason for each of us being here." Doug folds his hands, looks up, and flutters his eyes. "We are all here to help each other and save each other's souls. Bullshit. There ain't a person in the world who could die this minute and expect to slow me down. We weren't even *put* here. We just kinda *got* here. Now that we're here, only one thing for us to do—survive."

"You're entitled to believe what you choose."

"Oh, but you've got better answers, right?"

"I didn't say that. Most of what I've done I've done only for myself. I guess that's what you mean by survival. It hasn't made me very happy though, and it looks like it hasn't done much for you either."

That is enough to break Doug's stride.

"You know what I would do if I was hungry?" says Doug, trying to regain lost ground. "Really hungry? I would eat a rat. I'd sit one night in the kitchen and when he came out I'd zap him with a frying pan, put him in the pan and fry him up."

"You wouldn't be the first. At the end of the war the people in Tokyo had to eat rats."

Obviously unsettling news to Doug, who believed his fantasy had no actual precedent. The twins are touchy about it and positively insist the discussion end. They don't want to hear about a rat. They've heard scratching sounds at night.

Every night before midnight, sometimes much earlier if Maggie has passed out, Baggs leaves for the hospital. Doug has yet to return a good night or even call him by his given name.

One night, on his way out, Baggs stops at the sofa to ask a question. He wants to believe its purpose is to close the gap between Doug and him. The truth is that he would really like to know.

"Doug, what's the best way to kill a dude?"

Doug is up on an elbow, then against the armrest, then in an upright position. Now you're talking.

"Who wants to know?" asks the expert in such sinister treachery.

"There's this person I've been after for years. He was my company commander in boot camp. I want to kill him, only I never gave much thought to how I would do it."

"Shit, kill him. You want to kiss his ass, take him to Holy Communion."

"No, I really want to kill him."

"No jive?"

58

"You don't know this man."

"What's been in your way?"

"I can't find the mollywopper. But eventually I will, and then I'd like to kill him."

The gap is closing.

"Well, it all depends," says Murder, Inc., leaning forward. "First of all, does it matter to you if you get away with it or not?"

"All things equal, I would prefer to get away with it . . ."

"Now you're talking. It doesn't count if you can't get away with it. Make it look like robbery."

". . . but it's not a set requirement."

"Right. Second, does he have to know who's doing it?"

"By all means. No cutting corners there."

"Right. That means a frontal attack. Do you want him to suffer, or do you want it clean and quick?"

"Clean and quick, I suppose. I want him to know why, then *poof.*"

What a conversation to be having with a child!

"I like a knife," says Doug. "Feel your own ribs to give you an idea of how high to aim. If you can, right under the arm is okay, if your shank is long enough. Don't aim for the guts unless you want him to lie around hurtin' for a while."

"Where did you learn all this?"

"You got to know these things if you want to survive."

Lately, Baggs does not take it so much for granted that he does.

Though far from friendly, the studious killers at least can now exchange professional courtesies. When Baggs says, "Good night, Dougie," Doug is more times than not apt to say, "Yeah."

Baggs tries to champion the twins' cause against an insensitive teacher, but since he is locked up in the hospital during school hours he can offer only moral support. He quotes his benefactor Martin Luther, who once vowed he would never let any man drag him so low as to make him hate the man.

Baggs' hypocrisy is enough to make a prune out of his heart. From Doug he earns the title "Padre."

16

LIFE AT the hospital remains steady and sterile. The midnight padre weaves down its corridors and holds tight to the rail when the elevator blasts off. His stomach is a bonbon from Old Sly Fox, his sexual part weak from communion. His heart he tries to ignore.

He signs in at the medical station and routinely asks the ensign nurse, "Did they find my records yet?"

"Sorry, Baggs. I really am sorry; I'm not just saying that."

"Yes, ma'am, I know you are. Thank you."

Breakfast in bed and then the rounds of the other beds, collecting little boxes of cereal for Doug and the twins. Before Baggs, there was no cereal for breakfast. Often there was no breakfast at all.

The other patients believe Baggs is in some kind of black market food business.

He swabs down the deck and makes himself ready for the peering curiosity of the doctor. Baggs respectfully refuses all chocolate cysts, regardless of flavored toppings. *Ugh! Ugh! Ugh!*

Every four hours he joins several others for a sitz bath, dry in his case. The times they are a-changing: the sitzers pass around a joint. *Mox nix* to Baggs. He hits on it and passes it on as though enlightenment never had another source.

It's a whole new world out there, Ditty. Nobody wants to work for Eastman Kodak anymore. *Mox nix* to Baggs.

17

THE TWINS ARE skipping rope in someone's basement. Doug is on the streets practicing his supercool black strut. Baggs and Maggie are on the living room floor, his head on her belly. There is contentment.

"Jobs aren't so good there," she says, back on her favorite subject: knowing what it means to miss New Orleans.

"But it don't cost you all the blood in your body and your right tit for rent. We could get a place, the five of us, that we'd be tickled to live in, for sixty dollars tops."

"That sounds reasonable."

"In the Quarter."

"I've never seen it," admits Baggs.

"Then you got an eyeful coming you. This ain't no liberty at all here, compared to home, and I heard sailors say San Francisco don't even compare. Anything you want to get into, you can get into in New Orleans. And a phone call is still only a nickel."

"I got no one to call."

"You can get into anything."

"My problem is getting *out* of things."

"You wanna ride the bus or the trolley? Fifteen cents only."

"Let's ride it all day long."

"At night you don't so much *hear* the music as you can feel the vibrations lying there in your crib. There's windows in one of the dives that sing when the beat is hard enough. You can put your hands against them and get the music through your fingertips."

"I didn't know you liked music, Maggie."

"Who don't like music? I'll take you to Mom's Society Page Lounge. If you make it through that, I'll take you to another place. We'll have some fun for once in our sorry lives."

"This is as good as it gets until I can get out of the hospital. Then I'm going to do something for you and the kids."

"What I can't dig is if you're so all lost by the Navy in Portsmouth, how could you be any less lost in New Orleans? Hell's bells, you'd be *more* lost."

This is Maggie's way of considering the percentage of going over the hill. It startles Baggs because she is a fleet chick and should know better. Especially since she must realize that it's been on his mind too.

"The only thing stopping me is fear," he says.

She nods and says, "Fear ain't necessarily a belittlin' thing."

"They treat you discourteously when they find you."

"I know," she says, still nodding. "Aw, well, it'll all come out in the wash. Somethin'll shake loose eventually and we'll pack our bags."

What bags? Maggie has forgotten leaving them long ago in an unpaid hotel room.

"What do you think, Johnny: are you gonna hang around awhile?"

"Got nowhere else to go, Maggie, except to my reward."

There is a silence, and then she determines, "Dying is like leaving Bourbon Street and winding up north of the Mason-Dixon Line. Bourbon's been swinging every night before you showed up, and it'll swing every night after you're gone, even though you'll never swing with it again. Your ass is dead cold north of the Mason-Dixon Line where the windows never learned to sing."

"Maggie, you haven't made it north of the Mason-Dixon Line yet."

"Now you're bullshitting me."

"Sorry."

"You call this jug of piss the *South?*"

"I do and you don't, apparently."

"And here we are lying on the floor together with your elbow in my joint. The more you see, the less you know."

There comes a rap on the door. Maggie looks through the peephole, spins around, and presses her back to the door, her arms spread wide, as though the wolf has truly arrived. One minute it's bliss in New Orleans, the next, panic in Portsmouth.

"Get under the bed!" she hisses at Baggs.

"What?"

"Get the hell under the bed! Hide!"

An old boyfriend, thinks Baggs. He does not move. He suspects that no one has recently fought over his Maggie. Not since Mardi Gras of '56. Not since the sixth grade. Hell, no one's ever fought over Maggie in her whole life.

"Let him in," says Baggs.

"It's my goddam social worker!" she hisses.

"Watch your mouth. You expect me to hide under your bed out of respect for some bureaucrat?"

"Jesus, Johnny, we're out of two different worlds. We'll never reach New Orleans."

"Watch your mouth."

Baggs brushes her aside and opens the door. The woman carries a blue vinyl zipper bag and a weak smile of satisfaction.

"This is my brother from New Orleans, Miss Watkins. Brob-brob, meet Miss Watkins."

"I am not her brother, Miss Watkins."

"Yes, I thought you weren't."

"Miss Watkins," says Maggie, "ain't this a helluva way to spend your nights? Can't we get you a fella somewhere? Johnny, do you know a boy for Miss Watkins?"

She is inside the apartment now, and Baggs thinks she is looking for a clean place to sit.

"I don't enjoy this sort of thing," she says, "but neither do the taxpayers enjoy paying for welfare."

"I'm happy to report that nothing is too good for our fighting boys in uniform," says Baggs.

"Oh, shit," says Maggie.

Miss Watkins permits another weak smile and walks to the refrigerator as if it were her own. She opens it and stoops to examine its contents.

"Miss Paul, there's wine in here, and only half a quart of milk."

"The kids hate milk, and the wine is his. He brought it with him."

"I hope you haven't been misusing your food stamps."

"Would you like me to tell you where to paste your crummy food stamps?" says Maggie.

"Don't tell her, Maggie."

"I'll tell her."

But Miss Watkins will not hear it. She goes to the bathroom and opens the medicine cabinet.

"It's *my* razor!" yells Maggie. "I have to shave my friggin' legs, don't I? And what about my armpits?"

"Do you also splash them with Aqua Velva?"

"Well, what if I do? What if I *do?*"

But Miss Watkins ignores her. Maggie is used to it. She has learned this: it is the one called "client" who must clutch the gooey end of the stick.

Miss Watkins is now ready for Baggs.

"Are you assuming the role?" she asks him.

It is a new one on Baggs. There is an unmistakably official ring to it; it has the sound of an active process, something that has become part of a language, albeit esoteric.

The first association he makes is the one closest at hand. There is an order one hears many times a day at boot camp: "Assume the position."

Never with an exclamation point, shouted in anger, but always calm and calculated, delivered in total power, couched in anticipation of sadistic pleasure. The company commander is the one who says it, and sixty-eight men fall to the hard cold December Illinois ground and hold themselves above it by their toes and their outstretched hands.

If the company commander is short of breath he says, "Ready, be*gin.*" The men begin the push-ups and scream in unison, "*One,* sir, *two,* sir, *three,* sir, *four,* sir, *five,* sir, *six,* sir . . ." Around "Thirty-*two,* sir, thirty-*three,* sir. . ." you hear the few fatties in the company whining and you hear the company commander kick their asses that are sagging too low.

If the company commander is not short of breath, he will march them to the nearest snow and say in his acid voice, "Assume the position." Then he will say, "*One,*" smartly. Sixty-eight men lower their faces and chests and bellies to an inch above the snow. When the company commander says, "*Two,*" they may straighten out their arms again. But the fun for the CC is in leaving them in the number one position until they whimper and collapse. Then he can step their faces into the snow.

Baggs mastered assuming the position. He had a way of jamming an elbow into his ribs so that he was supported by the laws of physics rather than the strain on his biceps. He could stay in the number one position indefinitely and often used the time to go over the hill mentally. He would shake his peacoat up high to the eyes and tuck his chin into it and he was gone, on his knees somewhere, holding in his cupped hands like a basin of holy water the bare bottom of the girl of his dreams, lowering his face to touch deliverance with his lips.

More than once he was so far over the hill that he did not hear the command to move to position number two. Sixty-seven men up and Baggs down. This meant a foot under his chest to flip him to his back, where he could watch the menacing face of Lynn Forshay as he decided the appropriate torture.

There are only a few things worth dying for, thinks Baggs, but surely the final revenge against Lynn Forshay must be among them. The thought of it has taken him past many bad times, and it serves him well still.

Miss Watkins feels no need to clarify. She stares down Baggs until he returns from boot camp and says, "Beg pardon."

"Are you a man assuming the role of spouse?"

Still it makes no sense to Baggs and he stands as dense as the earth.

"He's a boy I know, for cryin' out loud," says Maggie. "Don't I have the right to know a boy? I don't get to drop in on people every night and go through their things, like some folks."

"Are you the father of her child?" asks Miss Watkins.

"Which one?" asks Baggs absurdly. He is not the father of anyone, save the old man he will become if he lives.

"The one she's carrying now."

The one she's carrying *now?*

"Thanks a lot, Miss Watkins," says Maggie. "You're a friggin' peach, you know that?"

"You're going to have another kid?" asks Baggs.

"Every seven years I make a little mistake. Is that such a bad record?"

His first romances were with girls who did not kiss on the first date.

"What are you contributing to the family's support?" asks Miss Watkins of Baggs.

Baggs thinks for a moment and says, "Well, the kids seem to like me. Except for Doug. Doug doesn't seem to like anybody very much."

"I meant money."

"Ah, they've lost my pay record. If they ever find it I'll have a bundle of money on the books. Then I can repay Maggie the five bucks she lent me."

"Good night, Irene," says Maggie and falls into a chair.

"She gives you money?" asks Miss Watkins.

18

THE UPSHOT IS that Baggs has made Maggie lose her welfare money and is coming dangerously close to making her lose her children as well. The state cannot give money to an unwed mother who in turn gives it to a single man assuming the role of spouse. On the other hand, it cannot allow minor children to starve. The only solution, Maggie reasons, is for the state to take the children away.

"Maybe I should let 'em," she says. "They don't stand a chance in life with me anyway, and without them hanging around my neck, who knows, I might still be able to shake something out of this old grab bag."

"You don't mean that, do you?"

"Oh, God," says Maggie, looking up at Him and squeezing her breasts, "it's a nightmare to be a woman."

"Watch your mouth," says Baggs, and then on God's behalf adds, "I'm sorry."

"You're sorry? What are you *do*ing here?"

"You'll wake the children."

"What are you *do*ing here in my bed?" she says even louder.

"I'll go."

"Lie down," she says. "You messed me up, now you got to help straighten me out."

"I didn't know you were pregnant, Maggie."

Maggie chooses not to discuss it.

"I thought we were friends," says Baggs. "You would have told a friend."

"Friends?" says Maggie, the larger part of her still working out the larger problem. "We're dead broke." She looks at him closely. "I had better-looking boys than you, buddy."

"Well, I'm sorry I'm not better-looking."

Baggs is learning that the apologetic posture may be the only one that means anything in a world so awry.

"Be sorry you ain't rich."

"Maybe you love me," says Baggs, like a birdsong on the moon.

She sits bolt upright. "Oh, fine, all I need now is to get in a conversation with you about love. Love is . . . love is . . ."

Love is a hot subject and anyone popular enough to get on a TV talk show is defining it. The air is oversweet with tender catchphrases of love. People are pasting them on their car bumpers. Big business is using them to sell deodorants, T-shirts, rubber stamps, candles, and coffee mugs. Third-string poets, tone-deaf songsters, and bantamweight novelists, all defining conclusively.

Baggs is going to finish for her. "Love is . . ." he begins, and she finishes for both of them. "Love is shit with sugar on it," she says.

He will not say otherwise. She is in a mood. Yet he hopes that she loves him. He does not know why. He does not believe he loves her, but then love is . . . love is . . .

19

BAGGS BELIEVES that in any significant ceremony one must toss something special into it, something that will serve as a ready reminder of the happy event.

To this end, neither of them wears any underwear when they are married in judge's chambers.

It was Baggs' idea and Maggie wasted no breath on it. She could think of nothing else but running into the district welfare office and flashing her valid marriage license at Miss Watkins, proof that she was now at last a lawful niece of her Uncle Sam and entitled to the PX, the commissary store, the medical clinic, and best of all, when Baggs goes to sea, an al*lot*ment. It is one of her favorite words. Al*lot*ment, the second syllable symbolizing largess. As nice and as warm as dog breath, that word.

Doug and the twins attend the wedding. Doug shakes his head from side to side in wonder that he has become associated with two such losers as his mother and her boyfriend. The twins, of course, are delirious and alternately giggle and pinch each other to keep from giggling.

Maggie is impatient to have it over with. Baggs smiles vacantly like a man who has lost it all, so what the hell. Tonight he will leave the wedding bed at eleven-thirty as he has left the illicit bed at the same time on previous nights. There is something beautifully irresponsible in what he does. Baggs must cling to the irresponsibility of his actions.

Standing before His Honor, Baggs glances idly over his

shoulder at the couples waiting for their turn, and his eyes meet those of a bride-to-be and they stay there. She is an American beauty, blond and blue-eyed, creamy-skinned, sparkling teeth, as delectable as tapioca pudding surrounding a dip of French vanilla. She's always been everything that Maggie never was. Baggs recognizes her from his adolescent fantasies behind locked bathroom doors. She was the girl for whom, in his imagination, he went over the hill while doing push-ups for Forshay.

Fate is cruel in its timing. They fall in love. It will be the only perfect and permanent love either will ever know.

Maggie must shove him with her hip to get him to respond to His Honor, and after he avows constancy he turns back to his one true love, who has waited for him. Love is . . . love is . . .

Baggs deliberately leaves behind his package of food scraps and then leaves his new family on the corner while he returns for it.

The love of his life is taking her vows. Neither of them pays any attention to the groom. Who is he? He doesn't exist.

She turns and looks at Baggs with eternity swirling in her wet eyes.

Yes, my darling, I am here and with you always.

They nod to each other like lovers, so slightly that no one else can see them nod, and then Baggs leaves the chambers.

He catches up with his new wife and kids and puts his arm around Maggie's shoulders. Trudy takes his hand; Judy grabs a fistful of his jumper; Doug walks half a block ahead, still shaking his head like a man who's just witnessed an avoidable auto accident.

"Love is . . ." says Baggs, "love is . . ."

"Listen, Johnny," says Maggie. "Look into getting me an ID card first thing tomorrow."

20

BAGGS' HEART is becoming cluttered, what with his achingly hopeless (but perfect) love for another's bride, his brutal passion for an end to Forshay, his fatherly pity for the kids, *his* kids now, and whatever it is he has for Maggie, what passes for love between two people who were wed long before they met.

The twins call him "Daddy." First time ever for them. "My daddy" on their lips is like "My wife" on his. Tomorrow at school the talk will all be of Daddy.

Doug hides it, but Baggs knows he is pleased, relieved at least. It is the end of the parade of sailors marching past his sofa. As they climb the stairs Baggs puts an arm around Doug's shoulders and says, "Home, son."

"Christ!" says Doug. The stairway is too narrow to shake off his arm.

"Watch your mouth."

"Daddy don't like curses," says Judy.

"Do you, Daddy?" asks Trudy.

It is Daddy all the day long. Daddy up the stairs, Daddy around the table, and Daddy to the cots in the kitchen.

Baggs bumps his ass and hits his head as he tucks them in, in their cramped kitchen.

"Have you had enough to eat?" he asks them. It has become a constant concern.

"Yes, Daddy," says Judy.

"Me too, Daddy," says Trudy.

Me too. Everychild's aspiration. Everyman's epitaph.

Next morning Baggs tells the nurses and corpsmen at the medical station that he has taken to him a wife and now would like to fill out the proper forms. They all look at him as though this were not possible. In a manner of speaking, it isn't.

He did not put in a chit.

"You have to put in a chit?" Baggs asks.

"Of course you have to put in a chit."

"No one told me that."

"Well, you didn't tell anyone you had to get married."

"I did not *have* to get married."

"Then why did you?"

"Look, I'm still entitled to a personal emotion."

"No one said you weren't. What you're not entitled to is to go get married like that without getting your chit approved."

Difficult enough to navigate are the channels for a chit. More difficult still is going against the current: getting permission for something you've already done.

Especially difficult in Baggs' case because so many of those in authority are embarrassed by his continuing presence. The man came into their hospital with a bit of redness and scar tissue on his postanal dimple. Since then double amputees, fractured vertebrae, and regenerated livers have come and gone.

Baggs mentions marriage to his examining doctor and the cystomaniac starts in on the familial category: the mother cyst, the daughter cyst.

Baggs enlists the aid of a sympathetic corpsman, though *all* are of course sympathetic, to run interference for him. Inside of a week he is able to see the XO.

It has not been a week of wedded bliss for Baggs because nightly Maggie pretends she is a Navy wife, bitching about the system, the puny benefits, the lack of human concern for dependents.

"When do I get to go to the PX?" she wants to know, though she doesn't have a dime in her jeans to spend there.

"Maggie, it's not all that it's cracked up to be, believe me."

"I want to see for myself."

She has the civilian's image of the PX, a glittering showcase of an infinity of quality items, all of them priced for the destitute: cigarettes, a dime a pack; lipsticks, four for a quarter; hair dryers, a buck apiece. She imagines that what she truly, really wants, what she longs for with melancholy as dry as sourdough, is given away free for the asking. Dusting powder.

Baggs is admitted to the XO's office, where he stands at attention and sounds off.

"Baggs, sir, YN2, on temporary duty off the USS *Begonia.*"

Can a wretch out of Devil's Island feel homesick for the place?

"Baggs?" says the XO. "Aren't you . . ."

"Yes, sir, I am."

The XO swivels on his chair and gives Baggs his profile.

"What can I do for you, Baggs?"

"Sir, it seems I'm in an unusual situation. . . ."

"You're not here to bellyache, are you?"

"No, sir, I'm not here . . ."

"Because I'll cut off your water right now. Each man in the Navy has to do what he's called upon to do. He doesn't have to be cheerful about it, he just has to *do* it. One candyass starts bellyaching and then another picks it up and another and before you know it we might as well trade in our hardware for tiddlywinks."

"Beat them into plowshares," suggests the padre.

"What? What?" asks the XO rapidly, suspecting a mutiny.

"You're right, sir. I agree. I'm not a bellyacher."

"Good man," he says, relieved. It won't happen on his watch. "What can I do for you, Baggs?"

"Well, sir, I got married last week."

The XO's eyes narrow. Anyway, the eye Baggs can see narrows. One narrow-eyed jack.

"Did you put in a chit?"

"No, sir."

The XO slams his palm against the desktop.

"Sorry, sir, I didn't know I was supposed to."

"That's about the assholingest excuse I ever heard. *Noth*ing's done without a chit."

"Sorry, sir."

Baggs believes it is the XO's turn to speak. He stands at attention waiting for the rigid profile to move. The silence is oppressive and Baggs says, "Sir, may I stand at ease?"

"What? No, I don't think so."

Baggs, who already began his move to the more comfortable position, snaps back to attention.

"Baggs, you have some education, don't you?"

"Yes, sir."

"Navy needs bright men with education."

"Yes, sir," says Baggs.

There must be something about the way he says it, for the XO swivels full front and demands, "What's that?" He sniffs the air for the putrid odor of mutiny.

"Yes, sir, I'm on my second enlistment."

"Giving us the benefit of your education, huh?"

"I was a physics major, sir."

"That's the ticket. These artsy-craftsy types are a dime a dozen. Give me physics any day."

"Yes, sir."

The XO brings ten fingertips together and leans back in his chair. "Baggs, my boy, why did an intelligent young man like

76

you with a background in physics go off and marry some down-town barroom whore?"

"Now, just a minute, sir, I must respectfully . . ."

"You must respectfully *shit.* Are you telling me you didn't marry a downtown whore?"

"She is not a whore, sir. She may have worked in a bar, but . . ."

The XO comes forward again. "But your butt. She's one of those champagne cocktail sippers, huh, buck and a half a throw, anything to separate a sailor from his dough."

"She doesn't work anymore. That all stopped when I met her."

"They should do a study on why so many intelligent good lads, clean lads in the Navy, wind up marrying so many cham-pagne-cocktail-sipping cock-teasing barroom whores. It's the craziest thing."

"Yes, sir."

Give it up, Baggs. Yes, sir, no, sir, thank you, I'm sorry—the four cardinal points of the compass.

We're talking about you, Maggie sweet, my destiny.

"She's going to have a baby," Baggs says, for something to say.

"Yours?"

Could it be? Once there was a Baggs who would have asked that question before all others.

"I'll ask her, sir."

"Oh, brother and Mother Machree," says the XO.

"All I want, sir, is to get her an ID so that she and the kids will be entitled to dependents' benefits. The boy has a mouthful of rotten teeth."

The XO swivels and gives Baggs his back.

"I know, sir, that I shouldn't bother you with this but I seem to be hitting a bulkhead everywhere else."

"Baggs, what you've done here is an extremely foolish thing. For all I know, it's a court-martial offense."

"Whom have I offended, sir?" asks Baggs incredulously, but he remembers that a sunburn at sea is also a court-martial offense, proof that one has been out of uniform and as a result has deliberately incapacitated himself, and to that extent has weakened the fighting force of a U.S. Navy vessel.

It is so difficult to tell what is apocryphal.

"You said kids," says the XO. "How many?"

"Three, sir, and the one on the way."

The XO sighs, looking out his window.

The hell with him, thinks Baggs, and he slides into at-ease.

"Baggs, sorry to say so, really am, but officially you are not married, not in the eyes of the Navy."

"Sir, in the eyes of Virginia and the rest of the world I sure am."

"Remember this: you may think you're in Virginia and you may think you're in the world, but what you're in is the Navy."

"Do you mean, sir . . ."

"You may take any stance on this matter that you please, but the fact is you are not married, nor can you *get* married without putting in a chit."

"Well, sir, I'll put in a chit."

"What good is that going to do you? You don't have any records."

"Do you mean I can't put in a chit if I don't . . ."

"Yes, and you can't get married unless you put in a chit."

"But then . . ."

"You're simply not married."

"Sir, I don't want to contradict you . . ."

"Then I would recommend, Baggs, that you don't."

"Yes, sir."

Attention, about-face. Like a sleepwalker he goes to Information and asks for Lost and Found. He leans into the window and tries to explain what's been lost. They call a corpsman, who leads Baggs to bed and gives him a shot of something.

Prompted by the shot, Baggs dreams of the Flying Seven in boot camp.

First, a singleton in the ass, pitched downward. The man in front of Baggs stepped forward with the needle still lodged in his buttock.

Step forward, pull up the drawers, and get your simultaneous air gun injections in each arm. If you flinch, the shot goes under the skin and travels around the arm, raising a blister like a bracelet that must be lanced and drained. Cry and they make you drink the stuff. Puke and they make you skate on it.

Step forward for a wiping, step forward for numbers four and five, needles this time, lower on the arms.

Forward for wipes, forward to the table at the end of the line. Lay both arms on the table for the two needles in the soft underpart of your forearms.

Your reward for maintaining consciousness throughout the Flying Seven is that the last two are given by nurses rather than corpsmen and they hold your hands for the instant it takes them to shoot you. They are ugly and their hands are cold, but what difference does that make?

Naturally, Lynn Forshay has been standing by the sidelines having himself a good cackle. *Die, Forshay, die!*

21

BAGGS, on his way to tell Maggie the bad news: her relationship to Uncle Sam is illegitimate. The only relationship of her life that is not is her marriage to John Baggs, as far as Virginia and the rest of the world are concerned.

He is stopped by two schoolgirls around Doug's age. One of them holds up a bar of candy like an oversized forefinger emphasizing a point. She says, "Buy a bar and save a boy?"

"Beg pardon?"

"There's a boy in our school, his name is Artie Montgomery, and he needs a dialysis machine right away or he's gonna die."

"I don't understand."

"He's got a kidney infection and he's gonna get a transplant, but he needs to get on this dialysis machine if he's gonna stay alive for the operation."

"Well, what's the problem? Why isn't he on a machine?"

"There aren't enough of the machines to go around and they're real expensive, and then he needs money so he can have the operation. So all of us kids at school are selling candy bars, fifty cents apiece. Buy one?"

"Or else he'll die?"

"We're also collecting Green Stamps. You can get a machine with Green Stamps."

It is the kind of cuckooity that makes Baggs feel faint.

"How much do you need?"

"Our goal is twenty thousand dollars."

"Or else he'll die?"

Baggs wants a straight answer to that one.

"Don't worry, we're gonna raise the money," one girl says with determination.

They are probably being encouraged in this. The effort has probably brought together friend and foe in a common cause: raise the loot to save a young boy's life. If they are successful, the President will probably commend them in a telegram. Has anyone thought of trading in one tiny bomb from the moldering stockpile of the things for a dialysis machine for little Artie Montgomery? Have his classmates and neighbors thought of asking the doctor and hospital to do it for free because little Artie is too young to die for the lack of twenty grand? Even the penniless Baggs sees it as an infinitesimal figure compared to the going price of an underground blast of the latest luxury-model bomb. Has anyone thought of skipping the next blast and giving Artie a nick of the action, just enough to get him a new kidney, so that we can all see what he would be like as a grown-up man? What about all of us just going down to the Green Stamp people and telling them to fork over a damn machine?

Baggs takes all the money out of his pocket and counts it. Thirty-seven cents.

He is inclined to give it to them, but something makes him say, "I'm sorry, I can't give you any money."

The two girls look at each other in disbelief. Their faces are full of disgust for Baggs' gunmetal heart.

"It may help Artie Montgomery," he says, "but what about the next kid, and the kid after that? Are they going to have to stake their lives on their neighbors' passing the hat for them? You're playing right into their hands."

"Whose hands?"

Baggs hastens away from them.

They shout after him, "I hope it happens to you!"

"I'm sure it will," he calls over his shoulder.

Near the apartment are two more girls, also hustling candy bars for Artie Montgomery. Baggs gives them his thirty-seven cents.

" 'Ja get it?" Maggie asks him before he can shut the door behind him.

"Where are the twins?"

"Playing," she says.

"Where?"

"Outside."

"*Mag*gie."

"They're all right, for Chrissake, they're only outside."

"Watch your mouth."

Doug comes out of the bathroom. He's been practicing looking tough.

"Doug, do you know Artie Montgomery?"

"I know him. He's not going to survive."

Baggs would like to know more about him, but Doug leaves. What's to know, anyway? He's underweight, he's becoming as good at dominoes as he once was at baseball. Does he curse his kidneys for impoverishing his family? Can he love his country?

"Well, 'ja get it yet?"

What'll it be, Maggie? The south of France, the north of Italy, the French Quarter of New Orleans?

The PX.

He tells her what's been told to him. The PX doors will not swing open for Maggie.

In a world chock full of inequities, how has Maggie cornered the market? Or as she puts it, "How come everybody gets chicken and I get feathers?"

She even cries, an act of weakness she disdains. She had plans to return to the PX repeatedly until she hoarded enough free

82

dusting powder to ensure a dry, scented crotch for the rest of her days. Is that asking so much?

"Believe me, Maggie, nothing is for nothing there. Oh, once in a while there may be some dude standing at the door handing out little packs of cigarettes, four in a pack, but that's about the extent of it."

She doesn't believe him.

She sobs, "I finally got me married a sailor, and for what? Nothing! I don't get nothing! I can't even go to the base movie, and all it costs is a *dime.*"

"Wipe your nose," he tells her.

"It sure don't take you long to start dishing out the orders."

"We'll find happiness outside of the base movie. Maggie, I'm going to be the only man who never hit you. You have my promise, I don't care what you do."

What does Maggie care? Talk sense, Baggs.

"Does this mean that if you go to sea I don't even get an allotment?" she asks, pretty sure that's what it means.

"If I go to sea, you'll get an allotment."

There is that at least. She lets him hold her.

"When will you be going?" she asks.

"You're not understanding. I can't go *any*where until they come up with my records. I'm stuck."

"Aw, Johnny, how the hell did I get in this mess? Of all the sailors in this town, why did I have to marry you?"

"We were meant for each other."

In her uncertainty she wants to hold the familiar handle. She unbuttons the front flap of his trousers.

"Look at you," she says, "standing here with a hard-on as big as the Ritz and you probably don't have two pennies to rub together."

"Not even one," he says, as though one could rub itself.

"Well, I guess it don't cost nothing for a hard-on."

"The best things in life are free," says Baggs.

"And look at me, I can't work now. We're all going to starve."

"God will provide," he says automatically.

She strokes him gently with her fingertips.

"Maggie?"

"What?"

"Would you ever categorize yourself as a champagne-cocktail-sipping downtown barroom whore?"

"Second generation," she answers simply.

You have to give executive officers some credit for insight.

"Maggie, this baby you're going to have?" he asks, following the deductions of the XO.

"What about it?" she asks suspiciously.

No one has ever mentioned an abortion. No one ever will.

Baggs hesitates and says, "What are you going to name it?"

"You can give it a name," she says, relieved.

Proof positive, but now from her own lips.

"Why? Why should I have that honor?" he asks.

"You're my old man, ain't you?"

Which isn't necessarily the same as being the baby's old man.

22

"WHY DO YOU think I married you?" becomes a frequent riddle around the Baggs place.

"Not in front of the children, Maggie."

The children can hardly care less. The twins still believe Baggs came to them from heaven, Doug still believes he walked in out of left field.

With her pride sticking in her teeth like popcorn, Maggie must lead her brood down to the district welfare office to seek out Miss Watkins to renew the dole. She gives her name to the clerk and sits to watch the others as the others watch her, measuring the degree of each other's need and sincerity.

It takes Miss Watkins half an hour to come down from her office on the third floor. Maggie shows her the marriage license and sits with her three in the cubicle while Miss Watkins dashes away to do some quick research.

The district office knows as well as bargirls what a YN2 receives in pay and benefits. Maggie is not qualified for aid.

Until she explains to them her husband's peculiar situation.

The concept of lost records is certainly not new to the district office. A manila folder is a frail uncertain thing in the Shanghai of any bureaucracy. But they have always been at the other end of it. They openly resent Maggie's involvement with Baggs and the subsequent involvement with the welfare office. They scurry back and forth, up and down, searching for a regulation and procedure to cover the case. Maggie can almost hear the computers snarling.

Here we have a man in the home, but not really *in* the home. An able-bodied man, employable except that he is already employed, earning nothing. A man unable to contribute dime one to the support of the children, and yet a stalwart in the service of the country.

"As I recall," says Miss Watkins, "he isn't even what one would call handsome, and he seemed somewhat dull mentally and emotionally."

"Please, Miss Watkins, I ain't up to it. Do I get the dough or do I cut my children's throats?"

It is not the kind of wisecrack to offer in a district office. They give her the aid anyway.

It is not enough to live on, but it will nicely postpone perishing.

Baggs must somehow take up the slack. It occurs to him that there has to be in Tidewater an employer who can use him during the hours of Cinderella liberty. He looks for a job, something he has not had to do since his teens. Now, as then, he is prepared to go for a kid's kind of job, at below the minimum salary, in cash, a job no one wants much, during hours that should be one's own. If he gets the job, he must keep it secret or Miss Watkins will deduct his earnings from their welfare. What's more, he must keep it secret from the Navy; to take a job is probably a court-martial offense.

Times is hard, he hears from all sources. The blanks he draws have been drawn before him by his stepson, Doug. In Doug's case, however, it was racial discrimination that closed the doors.

"An excuse," Baggs points out.

"What's your excuse, then?" asks Doug.

"Overqualification."

It is not as good as racial discrimination.

"Truth is, times is hard," Baggs tells his stepson.

And not likely to get better.

Maggie has come upon an ad that looks for a young, responsible man with evenings and weekends free. Baggs does not stop to define "weekends" but calls the number straightaway.

"We'd like someone with a year or two of college," says the soft voice of the receptionist.

"Four years, here."

"Oh, fine. Military experience?"

"Roger. U.S. Navy."

"Nights and weekends free?"

"That's me."

"Christian?"

"You betcha."

"White?"

"As the falling snow."

He arranges for a four-thirty appointment. He has had to arrange appointments for four-thirty in the past, which always worked a hardship on Baggs and his family because it made him miss chow at the hospital.

He borrows some decent civilian clothes from two men on the ward, a shirt here, mismatched slacks there.

No one has a tie, but a corpsman finds an officer's regulation black tie in the lucky bag and gives it to Baggs. There are no sport coats either, so Baggs wears over his shirt and tie a peacoat without insignia.

The outer office does not reveal the business of the inner office, and the crossed flags that decorate three of the four walls do not put Baggs at ease. You can fly any number of flags and still not be a fine fellow.

The receptionist buzzes her boss and then tells Baggs, "Colonel Gross will see you now."

If it has to be Gross, does it also have to be Colonel? wonders

Baggs as he rises to put his best foot forward. At least this is no kid's job, no sweaty kitchen or greasy burgers.

The man behind the huge desk pretends the papers in front of him are more important than the entry of the applicant.

Baggs notices the colonel is in uniform, but from his angle and distance he is unable to say what kind of uniform. He shuts the door behind him and stands still and silent, wondering should he clear his throat.

No need to. The colonel acknowledges him and rises to step around the desk for a shake of the hand.

Baggs sees now that Colonel Gross is wearing a Boy Scout uniform.

As he shakes Baggs' hand, he tugs at his shorts with the other hand to bring them down from their sitting position. Baggs cannot take his eyes away from the colonel's neckerchief holder: a hand-carved wooden Indian, painted purple, who appears to be hanging onto the neckerchief with both arms and legs and peeking over the juncture of the two rolls of kerchief, his disproportionate nose foremost.

Having shaken Baggs' hand the normal way, Colonel Gross extends his hand again, this time lowering his little finger away from the others. In an instant it all comes back to Baggs and he extends a like hand, connecting slot to slot in the Boy Scout handshake.

"Ah, ha!" says the colonel.

Baggs is now a serious candidate.

Take the offensive, Baggs. He flashes the Boy Scout salute.

With military bearing and a comrade's smile the colonel returns the salute.

"Have a seat, Mr. Baggs."

The colonel sits informally on the edge of his desk, his khaki shorts once again cutting into his hairy legs. He adjusts his knee socks and properly aligns the tassels that hang from the garters.

88

Baggs is overdue for a long, honest, fulfilling laugh, but he bites his tongue to keep the roar from smashing out of his body. He wants the scoutmaster job; it will be a plum. Develop a rapport with the boys and they'll cover for you. Baggs plans his first innovation as scoutmaster: to each meeting each boy will bring a can of food for the poor people. Cash will also be acceptable. Baggs sees an end to his family's hunger. Thanks be to God.

"How far did you get in the Scouts?" inquires the colonel.

Baggs gives himself an impromptu promotion.

"Star," he says.

It wouldn't do to confess that after all those years he never rose higher than first-class scout. Baggs didn't really care for the Boy Scouts; it was just another thing you had to do as a small boy in a small town.

The colonel looks disappointed.

"I had rheumatic fever and it slowed me down," lies Baggs.

"Ah, tough break," says the colonel, pleased at the explanation. "How are you feeling now?"

"Fit as a fiddle and rarin' to go," says Baggs, leaning forward and rubbing his hands together.

The colonel moves his arm and thrusts out his chest a bit. Baggs picks up the clue immediately.

"And you, sir? How far did you go?"

Colonel Gross smiles. "Only as far as you *can* go."

Baggs shakes his head in awe.

"At one time I was the youngest Eagle in Torrance, California."

Baggs adds commendatory audio to his head-shaking.

"But enough of this reminiscing. You're here for a job, right?"

"Right, sir. You know, I have a boy of my own, thirteen years old. He's my stepson, but we're like this."

Baggs raises his crossed fingers. He wants to indicate to the colonel that he can attract new blood to the troop. He will have to figure out some way to make Doug leave his shiv at home.

The colonel, however, seems confused by Baggs' remark. Finally he says, "Married man, huh?"

"Yes, sir. Three kids and another in the oven."

"Terrific! You want to make some money?"

For a moment Baggs is nonplussed. He expected money to be the last subject mentioned and then in an apologetic way, calling to mind the many nonmonetary rewards of leading a troop of scouts.

"Well, yes, yes, sir, I would."

"You've come to the right place."

The colonel gets up and walks to a cabinet against the wall. The ubiquitous crossed flags, half-size in this case, are poised above the cabinet. The colonel reaches inside and comes back to Baggs turning the base of a lipstick, revealing an inch of pink that at sea would cause Baggs to vomit.

He shoves it in front of Baggs' nose and asks, "Do you know what this little item retails for?"

Baggs takes the lipstick and inspects it.

"No, sir."

"Two ninety-nine. We can't keep enough in stock. Do you know what it costs to make one? Twelve cents. I got hundreds of Filipinos making the casings out of old beer cans."

"I don't get it," confesses Baggs.

"What's to get? You make a piece of shit for twelve cents and sell it for two ninety-nine. I've got salesmen across seven eastern states and expanding every day. There's a good career for a young man in cosmetics."

"Cosmetics?"

"I'm embarrassed to tell you what the margin of profit is on mascara."

"You're not in Boy Scouts?"

"Boy Scouts? I'm sixty years old, for crying out loud."

Baggs bites his tongue again. At the very least there may be a sample case for Maggie in it. But it's no use. The roar rushes out of Baggs. It is enough, almost, to roll up the colonel's carpet and flutter his flags.

In recalling the experience for Maggie and the kids, Baggs can vaguely remember the colonel pummeling him about the head and shoulders.

23

BAGGS, shopping at the PX for Forshay. Also for a can of shaving foam.

If he finds Forshay, he will not have to stage a robbery to cover up the murder; he will in fact rob him. Baggs has been unable to find civilian employment. He needs money. The need of it has made him impotent once. That and bringing to bed the humiliation of pleading with strangers for a job. They all have the same cocky stance, the same condescending smile, the same belittling questions, the same thirst for supremacy.

Forshay is not in stock, but he finds the shaving foam and at the cashier's counter counts out the price in dimes, nickels, and pennies cadged from the men on the ward.

He drops the last penny on the counter, daring the cashier to discover deep in his peacoat his cache of stolen treats for the kids. In Baggs' mind is the question of whether or not it is even possible for the Navy to court-martial him and send him to the brig without records. In his heart is the fear of once there, never to leave.

Thirty-nine cents and still another sin, but every kid deserves a sweet once in a while, whatever his circumstances.

Except Doug, who will split his candy into two and give half to each twin in exchange for future services. Baggs will believe it is because the gift came from him. He does not realize that candy on Doug's rotten teeth is torturous.

Baggs pauses at another PX island and thinks about ripping

off a small bottle of perfume for Maggie. Every woman deserves a bit of sweet smell now and again.

He is amazed at how facilely he makes his own rules.

A lieutenant on the other side of the island has a wary eye on Baggs.

Tomorrow or the next day, Maggie, we'll get you smelling sweet.

Baggs walks away. The lieutenant, however, is behind him and he says, "Just a minute, sailor."

Baggs, the very common thief, stops and like the rest of his brethren is happy to be caught at last. His soul has already begun to serve the bad time.

He turns around to surrender to the lieutenant.

The officer is smiling in a friendly way. It takes Baggs an extra beat or two to recognize Andy Warwick, an old Lambda Chi brother. His first thought is that if he could be crossing paths with Andy Warwick in Norfolk—the sailors' Forty-second and Broadway—so far away from college life that it is already a fuzzy memory, can Lynn Forshay be far away?

"I'll be damned," says Andy, extending his hand.

"Small world," says Baggs, shaking it.

Andy Warwick looks again at Baggs' YN2 chevrons. Warwick never imagined he would so outrank a contemporary.

"I'll be damned," he says.

In school Andy Warwick always wore a mock turtleneck sweater under his shirt. It was said he had to: he had a mock neck.

"It's the damnedest thing I ever heard of. Everybody wondered what the hell ever happened to you. You know, it was a real slap in the face to the house, dropping out like you did without a by-your-leave-sir."

The finest thing that ever happened to Andy Warwick was

being formally invited by a swell bunch of guys like the Lambda Chis to join their house. Ever afterward his behavior was predicated on what the house might think of him. Baggs joined because they were known to be the campus cocksmen. He was the only pre-theo in the house.

"Well, I had some personal problems; you know how it is."

"Why didn't you come to the brothers? We would have helped you work them out."

Baggs shudders, remembering their weekly group encounters. Like a pack of wilderness dogs they waited for the weakest of them to fall; then they tore him to pieces.

"You're in a sailor suit, an enlisted man," observed Andy Warwick.

Apparently he has not changed much. He was always a vague, ill-defined fellow who asked questions of his brothers that ranged from maddening to otherworldly. For example, he would come into Baggs' room while Baggs was sewing a button on a shirt and he would ask, "Are you sewing a button on your shirt?"

In a bad mood, one could find Andy intolerable, as Guts the wrestling jock did one morning when Andy inquired if he was brushing his hair. Guts pushed him out of the window and held him aloft by one ankle, pulling him back inside only after the other brothers convinced him that he would lose his scholarship if he dropped Warwick to the peonies three stories below.

Once Baggs, Andy, and two other brothers stopped at a diner on their way back to the campus after a basketball game at Hofstra. None of them had ever been in the place before. They sat in a booth reading the menu and Andy Warwick looked at the waitress, busy behind the counter, and said, "Oh, is she here?"

Baggs and the other two crossed their eyes and strummed their lips with their forefingers. The next week Warwick complained to the assembly of brothers about guys making fun of him. Everybody had second helpings of him. It was Warwick's darkest hour.

"You're a lieutenant," says Baggs, not surprised to find himself assuming Warwick's style. Since losing his records, his only true proof of existence, Baggs, chameleonlike, adopts the characteristics of those in closest proximity. He is an overgrown child with the twins, a killer with Doug, a lush and a lover with Maggie. With Andy Warwick he becomes a vacuity.

Andy gives his gold bars a quick brush with the end of his sleeve.

"How's that?" he says, pleased with himself.

"Fine," says Baggs.

"You never got your degree, huh?"

"Nope."

"Too bad. You could have been an officer too."

"No, no, I couldn't have. I could never be an officer."

This unsettles Warwick. He wouldn't dream of being an enlisted man, yet he is made sleepless by the idea that they have more fun than officers. He lies awake in his stateroom imagining the delightfully gross things they are doing on the beach. *Do* they really have more fun, on less pay and fewer benefits? It is a question he would like answered once and for all, and now with a hand firmly on Baggs' shoulder he has the opportunity to talk to an enlisted man he can talk to, a Lambda Chi like himself.

"Do you know what I'm going to do?" asks Andy Warwick.

Baggs thinks for a moment. "I give up."

"I'm going to buy you lunch, that's what."

It is Saturday and Baggs has had lunch at the hospital, but he will have another on Warwick and put it into paper sacks for the family.

They leave the PX together and outside Andy says, "Imagine, old fraternity brothers meeting like this after all this time and now here's one a full lieutenant and the other's an enlisted man."

Warwick does not have to spell out the scenario for Baggs, who can recognize the irony of it for himself, but Andy Warwick has always been an essayist on the obvious. Attend a wake with him and he will be certain to point out that the man in the coffin is dead. His only original contribution to Baggs' education was his proving conclusively that body gas is combustible. Baggs paid off a pack of cigarettes on the bet and thought the demonstration well worth it, but then, like a laboratory rat, Warwick kept returning to Baggs' room every time he felt the urge, rocking on his back on Baggs' bed, lit match in hand, waiting. If successful, he expected a reward of a cigarette, which Baggs would give the human flamethrower to get rid of him. A conditioning occurred, Baggs could never be sure to whom.

"I'd like to buy you lunch at the Officers' Club, but you being an enlisted man . . ."

"I understand."

"Everything over there is protocol."

"That's as it should be."

Warwick steps back so as to see him better.

"You know, John, you've grown up in the Navy."

"Thank you."

Scratch your head, Baggs; you're a nigger and you know it. Though Andy can go anywhere, you know your place. Grouse a little and they'll remind you of your three squares a day and a flop and your uniform that admits you to the USO where you can be with your own kind. Do your job well, that's important, but goddam, boy, you be there at the quarterdeck in your sparkling whites with the other sideboys when the brass comes aboard. Snap to, look good, make 'em feel important. Fetch coffee, pick up the old man at his house, pilot his gig. Look

96

good, dammit. Comes liberty call go get your pussful in the dark and loud places all you boys go to. Don't you fret about coming aboard feet first, carried up the gangplank. The old man'll look down at you and laugh and say, "I like to see my boys enjoying themselves." But God save you, boy, if you don't have your white hat on your head. What roaches? My God, boy, we're giving you more money than what's good for you. Keep yourself clean, speak when you're spoken to, and, boy, don't let the sun set on you in Officers' Country. And don't never line your ass with broken glass, 'cause the skipper's already circumcised.

"Well, look," says Andy Warwick, "what I'd like to do is go eat where all you guys eat, in one of those whaddayacallems."

"Gedonk."

"Right, a gedonk. Let's go eat in a gedonk."

They love to use the enlisted man's words, like politicians after the minority vote.

There is a long line there, as always, and Baggs stops at the end of it, but Warwick leads their way to the head of the line, saying, "Gangway—officer, gangway—officer."

The men can do nothing but move aside and let the hatred glow in their faces like hot briquettes. Somebody whispers into Baggs' ear as he walks by, "Pussy!"

There's never been a fragging in Norfolk, Baggs assures himself as he takes his tray and moves along the food line. He orders four cheeseburgers and soup. The soup is for him, the rest will go into the sack.

"Wow, what an appetite!" says Warwick. "You enlisted men really can eat."

In order to keep up their enormous sexual prowess.

Andy orders a tuna fish on white.

"I don't eat much," he says. "Officers never eat much. Drink the hell out of coffee, though."

To prove it, he drinks three quick cupfuls and has to go to the head. When he returns he says, "There was even a line at the urinals. I told them gangway. You guys stand in a lot of lines, huh?"

"For everything. One night I stood in line for a girl."

"No kidding? Where was this?"

"Old San Juan."

"No kidding? I bet you guys get laid every time you turn around. You been to the Med?"

"Sure."

"I bet you got laid in every country."

"Sure. All it takes is the price."

"It's different when you're an officer. Officers never get laid. It's all protocol; you can't be seen in the kind of place where you guys find all the good whores. You know how many times I got laid in the Med? Once. In Cannes, and it cost me a hundred bucks."

"It usually costs me five."

"Oh, man, what I wouldn't do for shore leave with some of you guys!"

"We call it liberty."

"You guys know how to live. Officers have a hard life. We have all the responsibility. That's why you never hear us singing."

"It's not all hand-clapping and foot-stomping in our corner, Andy."

Warwick looks around him uncomfortably.

"Better call me Mr. Warwick, John. Somebody might hear."

At one of the fraternity house dances Baggs told a girl Andy was trying to make time with that Andy's entire scalp was tattooed with the Book of Revelations and that this was only one small manifestation of his religious fanaticism. For the rest of the evening she leaned close to him and several times ran her fingers through his dark hair. Her attempts to scan Revelations were interpreted by Andy to be ardor.

"I'm afraid I'll never be able to call you mister, Andy," says Baggs.

Andy again looks to see if anyone has overheard the familiar form of address.

"Baggs, I can make you call me mister. It's as simple as your sleeve and my hat. You've got to call me mister. It's in the book."

Baggs rises to leave. The tab for the free lunch has run too high.

"Please sit down, John. I'm sorry. I really am. I don't know any enlisted men up close. I try to make friends with them, but I don't know how to get through to them. If you're nice to them, they take advantage. The guys in my division make fun of me."

Baggs sits down.

"It would help if you stopped thinking of me as an enlisted man and yourself as an officer," he says.

"Protocol, John. You can take the uniform off the man, but you can't take the man off the uniform."

Baggs gives him a moment, should he want to run through that one more time. When it's clear he will not, Baggs says, "I understand anyway."

"Don't address me at all. Don't call me anything."

"That's probably best," says Baggs.

Andy nibbles his sandwich, looking around him to see how the other half lives.

"Who would have thought when we were sitting around the frat house having our bull sessions that someday you and me would be sitting in a gedonk in Norfolk, Virginia?" asks Andy Warwick.

"No one," Baggs tells him.

"Life has many turns."

"It's a Chinatown."

"That's what keeps it interesting," observes Andy Warwick.

"Never a dull moment."

Andy slaps his forehead. "I forgot to even ask you. Are you married?"

"Yes."

"Really? Is she a Navy wife?"

It is a typical Warwick question. Baggs gives him a typical Baggs answer.

"Yes and no."

Valid question, complete answer.

"And you?" asks Baggs.

It is what Andy has been waiting for.

"Brother, am I ever married. Two kids."

"I've got three."

Andy slaps Baggs' arm. "Go on! Three?"

"Actually, they're my wife's children by a previous . . . something or other."

Warwick shows no curiosity. Instead he begins what Baggs believes must be his well-rehearsed story of how he came to join the Navy. He raises his voice, in case any of the other enlisted men have been wondering.

"I had a good job with a cement concern. Mucho room for advancement. On my first vacation in two years Marion and me and the two barfies were going to drive across the country in this Rambler I picked up for three hundred dollars. I should mention that Marion is a kind of S-type person, but I am not, nor have I ever been, an M-type person. The kids take after her, but that's another story. Let me just tell you it was not the crowd to travel across the country with in a used Rambler, which had a number of birdies in it that we were all used to. But there we are, traveling across New Mexico, doing about seventy per when we all hear the sound of a new birdie in the Rambler, which slowed considerably, from like seventy per to nothing on the side of the road. I can tell you there wasn't smile one anywhere in that car.

"All right, a hot day, a dead Rambler packed with everything but the goldfish. Everybody's on my neck. Way off in the distance I can see a turnoff, so I leave them in the car and I begin to hike, along the way thinking there must be a better life somewhere. At the turnoff there's an intersection and a sign: *West Cactus, 2 miles; East Guava, 2 miles.* So I stood there and hitchhiked with a thumb in each direction, what the hell. But there wasn't any traffic in either direction. So I said to myself, 'If I were looking for a square deal, where would I go, West Cactus or East Guava?' I finally chose West Cactus, and a wise choice too, because when Harry K. Square and Philip K. Deal were only kids they had this dream of becoming partners in a gas station. Harry was a three-pump kid in a two-pump station, and Phil used to stuff transmissions with bananas in a used-car lot. *Se Habla Español.* So they pooled their resources and opened up a station right there in West Cactus, N.M. They were going to call it the Deal and Square Garage, but an old maid aunt suggested they call it the Square Deal Garage. The rest is history.

"Now, the car is towed in. Big deal. Put it on the credit card. So I ask the mechanic, 'What's the problem?' 'Listen, Mac,' he tells me, 'it's five o'clock Friday. I'm goin' to have a few cold ones and then I'm goin' home.' I told him it would be worth a five-spot to me to have the car taken care of. 'Look, Mac,' he says, 'I been workin' garages for two years and nobody ever got me to work after Friday five o'clock.' I told him I'd go as high as ten bucks to have the car looked at now. Nothing doing. I tried to go to the top—Harry K. Square or Philip K. Deal—

but they made so much money they never came around the station anymore."

Baggs is growing restless and fidgets in his seat.

"Okay, I'll cut it short. I had to give the kid twenty-five dollars to tell me that they'd have to fly in the parts from Albuquerque and it would cost me about five hundred dollars to fix up the Rambler. Creative kiting, they call it. The desert states have a contest going. Never drive west in an automobile, John. To cut it short, I made a gift of that Rambler to Harry K. Square and Philip K. Deal, and I got a ride downtown, where I signed up for OCS. They sent me to Rhode Island and Marion and the kids to her mother's. And, brother, am I ever grateful. I see them three months or so out of every year. We're a happy family again. So that's my story."

"I wonder what ever became of the Rambler," says Baggs.

Andy looks at Baggs' empty tray and asks, "Finished with your lunch?"

"Who, me?"

Fire with fire.

"Cigarette?"

Tailor-mades. Baggs takes two, puts one behind his ear. Andy is about to light Baggs' cigarette, but instead lights his own and slides the pack of matches across the table to Baggs, saying, "Better light it yourself, John."

"Right," says Baggs, striking a match.

"I'd like to know how you wound up in your situation," says Andy.

"I'd like to know myself."

"I mean, you had it all going for you—a scholarship, good grades, dean's list."

"Only three times out of seven semesters."

"*Only*? One semester I took two art appreciation courses and

102

one music appreciation course and I *still* couldn't make the dean's team."

"Well, you know how it is: people change."

"But with all you had going for you, to wind up a YN2 . . ."

"It's an honest living."

"I never figured you'd make it as a preacher, none of us did, the way you used to booze and chase pussy."

"I didn't wear my religion on my sleeve, that's for sure."

"But I figured you'd get a good job with industry. You were so close to your degree."

"Nobody wants to work for industry anymore."

"Now here you are, a YN2 with a hash mark yet. You actually reenlisted."

A hash mark is a diagonal stripe on the forearm sleeve. Each one indicates four years of service.

Baggs raises his arm to look at the hash mark. "You're right," he says.

"Why? I'd like to know why, John, why?"

Should he try to tell him? Or should he simply smile secretively?

He smiles secretively.

"C'mon, John, we're friends and fraternity brothers; you can tell me."

Baggs puts his elbows on the table and leans confidentially toward Warwick.

"I'm having the time of my life," he whispers.

"I knew it! You're doing this crazy thing for the *fun* of it. Aw, man, you guys . . . I know you guys, you guys have all the fun. Boozing and whoring and everything."

"If I had as many on me as I been into, I'd look like Swiss cheese. I don't think my thing's been soft for more than eight hours running since I enlisted."

"Oh, man . . ."

"And then do you know what all us guys do when we're with ourselves?"

"What? What?" demands Warwick, disgusted with the meagerness of the officer's share of carnal joy.

"Get drunk and fall down in the dirt, roll around."

"In your uniforms and everything?"

"In the class A whites. Right in the dirt, roll around and kick each other with our heels."

"Man, you guys got it made," says Andy. "One night in the Med I was officer of the deck when the guys were coming back from liberty. You should have seen those guys, staggering and helping each other up the gangplank, full of *esprit*. You know what one of 'em told me? He said he got a haircut, manicure, shoeshine, and blow job, all without ever leaving the barber's chair."

"I been in that barbershop," says Baggs.

Andy Warwick grabs his arm. "Take me on liberty with you, Baggs, please?"

"I'd like to, Andy."

"But?"

"Well, you being an officer and everything. The guys wouldn't go for it. They've got—I don't know—pride."

"Aw, c'mon, you could explain it to them, fix it up. Maybe get me a gob outfit . . ."

"You would wear an EM's uniform?"

"Well, if the guys would be sore about me being an officer."

"That's an offense, Warwick, you shit."

Andy nervously looks around him.

"What kind of officer would wear an EM's uniform just so he could get laid and roll around drunk in the dirt?" Baggs raises his voice. "You must be some kind of a shit, Andy."

Andy's head is a spinning top.

"Keep it down, John, for God's sake, what are you trying to do to me? I'll be up for a command soon."

Baggs relaxes and says, "I suppose we could all go out in civvies."

"Why didn't I think of that? I'll get me a wrinkled sport shirt and some chinos."

"Be sure to carry a bottle of apple wine in a brown paper bag."

"You got it!" says Andy and gives him some skin.

"Only it won't be the same."

"What the hell. It'll be close enough."

"I'll talk to the guys about it."

"Oh, man, oh, man. Don't tell them we went to college together."

"I'll tell them we were in the slammer together. That'll impress them."

"Too much! I miss those wonderful days back at the house, John, when we could act so crazy and nobody would give a hoot. Don't you?"

"Having too much fun to look back, Andy."

"You son of a gun, you!"

Baggs folds over the end of his paper sack and makes ready to leave.

"Andy, I'm flat broke. Could you give me five bucks?"

"Do you guys do that, borrow money from each other?"

"Sure, all the time."

"Don't you know it's against Navy regs to borrow or lend money?"

"I'm asking you to *give* it to me."

"You won't pay it back?"

"Well, maybe I will."

"Wow," says Andy, "an officer giving money to an enlisted man. Wow, I wonder if that's ever happened before. I'm going to do it. I'll put it here on the table like it was a tip, and you pick it up when I'm not looking."

Andy Warwick is on the *Bradshaw,* a destroyer. Baggs tells him he is on the *Begonia.* They shake hands in parting outside the gedonk in full view of enlisted men coming and going. Someone mutters, "Cunt!" at Baggs.

24

DOUG TAKES the paper sack from Baggs and carries it to the kitchen as the twins take off Baggs' shoes, turn on the news, and bring him a sip of Old Sly Fox. Maggie is stretched out on the sofa, her hands on her swollen stomach.

"Been drinking?" he asks her.

"No."

"Good girl. It'll poison the kid. I brought you a cheeseburger."

This is great news to the kids, but Maggie says, "You eat it. I ain't hungry."

"You've got to eat, for the baby's sake. I bet you haven't eaten all day. The baby will be hungry."

"If I ain't hungry, the baby ain't hungry."

Baggs sighs. She has had three and he is only a man, not yet father for the first time.

"I have a creepy feeling," she says.

"Do you feel sick?"

Baggs, of course, has not witnessed a single morning sickness from his wife. This and the realization that he has never shared breakfast with his children cover him with sadness like a mudslide.

"I think I'm going into labor tonight," says Maggie. "Either that or I'm coming down with a cold."

"It's only been seven months," says Baggs.

"You can have a kid after seven months," yells Doug from the kitchen.

"He's right," says Maggie.

"Well, *I* know he's right," says Baggs, "only it's not the normal way to do it."

As though either of them were acquainted with doing things the normal way.

Maggie puts the back of her hand over her forehead. Baggs watches her and the evening news alternately.

"The burgers are warm," yells Doug.

The twins need no special invitation.

"Oh, my, oh, *my,*" says Maggie, who gets off the sofa and squats slightly. There at the crotch of her Goodwill Bermudas is a wet spot. "I broke my water," she says.

Baggs is on his feet. "Are you sure?"

"Well, I didn't pee my pants."

"What do we do now?" he asks, putting himself at her disposal. He knows none of this.

He helps her into the bathroom. The children are so occupied with their cheeseburgers they do not notice. He holds her steady and helps her take off her Bermudas and ragged panties. She holds a towel to her crotch. In a moment she drops the towel to the floor and takes a fresh one from the rack. Baggs bends down and picks up the wet towel. He sniffs at it and recognizes the odor, though he has never smelled broken water before. It is the brinish smell of man's beginning, with a trace of the medicine of nature, and a whiff of pure *woman.* The smell of it flings him back to Adam.

He touches the wetness to his tongue. It is the sea. Maggie sees him do it and she screws up her face. Silently he passes the towel to her. Initially reluctant, she finally smells it. She too puts her tongue to it. They look at each other, as close as they are apt to be.

Tough Maggie is so soft now as she touches him. He draws her head to his chest.

She wants a straight-back chair, which he gets for her. Together they sit in the bathroom, she on a towel on the chair, he on the edge of the bathtub, holding her hand.

"What do we do now?" asks Baggs.

Maggie smiles and says, "We cut out hot baths and sex."

Baggs smiles back and says nothing.

"Johnny," she says, "you've got a way about you."

They have had no prenatal care; it has been: do what you think is right. Without money or insurance no hospital arrangements could be made, so Baggs has planned to take her to Saint Mark's as near as feasible to actual birth and simply see if those Christians will turn them away or take them in.

The contractions never develop a pattern. They are twenty minutes apart, twelve, four, fifteen, two. Baggs leaves the bathroom to explain to the children what is happening. Can they go to the hospital too? they ask. Yes, that is part of the plan. In the meantime, Mother needs privacy, like a cat. They understand about cats.

Baggs and Maggie are in the bathroom for nearly two hours before she says, "I think we better make it now."

Baggs gives her a quick sponge bath and kisses her belly for luck before helping her dress. The children have been ready and waiting. Together they leave the apartment and walk to the corner bus stop.

The wait is short, ten minutes. The children board first. Baggs helps Maggie up the high first step.

"We're going to Saint Mark's Hospital," Baggs tells the driver as he pays the fare.

"The main thing is not to get excited," advises the bus driver.

The other passengers, however, cannot be casual about it. Nothing much ever happens aboard a bus. The customary excitement is a drunken sailor throwing up, and all would be happy never to have to see that again.

"It'll be a boy," says one middle-aged woman. "I'm psychic about these things."

A man leans toward Baggs and whispers, "You should of took her in a cab. This bus makes lots of stops."

It does make many stops, but Maggie tells Baggs not to worry. Judy and Trudy brief each new boarder on the drama now in progress.

Everyone wishes them well when they get off at the hospital, and the ride has made a random group of strangers feel warm toward each other.

There is some difficulty at the reception desk. There is no way to explain the absence of an admitting or attending doctor, and although Baggs tells the cashier a good story about being caught two months early on a weekend, not yet having transferred funds, it is no secret that a family of deadbeats has crashed the gates. On their own cue, the twins send up a wail, and soon Maggie is rolled away on a wheel chair to be prepared for offering up another life to the world.

Baggs fills out the forms, and then like conspirators who have gone so far so good, he and the kids wait in the visitors' lounge.

Soon a nurse comes and asks Baggs if he would like to be with Maggie in the labor room. Baggs assumed he must keep the vigil in the lounge, and would prefer to, actually, but he does not decline the invitation.

"Okay, Dougie, you're in charge. Judy and Trudy, you listen to Doug. I want you guys to stay here till this is over. You can go to the gedonk for doughnuts if you get hungry, but come right back here and don't go exploring."

He gives them the change in his pocket and goes with the nurse.

In the room there is a doctor examining Maggie. He introduces himself, but Baggs immediately forgets his name. Baggs looks at the wall clock. It is nearly nine o'clock.

"How long, do you think, doctor?" he asks.

"It would have been better if the water had broken later in the labor," says the doctor, but he is light and puts Baggs at ease.

The doctor leaves, a nurse checks often, but mostly Baggs is alone with Maggie, comforting her through the frequent and painful contractions. Beads of sweat form on his brow, and Maggie says, "It seems worse than it is. It ain't that bad. It's no worse than crappin' out a rockin' chair."

Maggie, simple giver of life. Before long the world will change because someone is coming. The arrival, sojourn, and departure of the new visitor will change the world, to a lesser or greater degree, but to *some* degree.

Baggs has forgotten that the visitor will be *his* child, and when he remembers again it occurs to him that it will be *everybody*'s baby, and consequently Baggs is every baby's father, especially this one's father, whether of his seed or another's.

It is a simple and basic truth, and he is angry at his own ignorance for having to wait to become a father to learn what he should have learned as a son, which once learned ends war.

It is eleven-thirty before Maggie is asked to push. Baggs and the nurse each hook an arm around one of Maggie's legs and pull back as she pushes. The minute hand is on the upward swing. Baggs has never been AWOL before, but he sees no way to avoid it now. The nurse directs her flashlight between Maggie's legs and says, "I see it. It has black hair."

She gives Baggs the flashlight and tells him to look for himself. He's been there so often and has rested hand, head, and core against it, but never has he really looked at it, naked and furless, under direct light. Now that he does, he sees again something from the sea, clamlike, tired of darkness, seeking the light. He looks away but says for her benefit, "I see it, Maggie, it has black hair."

Well, so does Maggie, very dark brown anyway. Baggs is fair, his hair almost blond. Maggie's is probably closer to medium brown. Light brown, if she's been out in the sun for a while. Fact is, she's about a shade lighter than Baggs.

The doctor is back in the room and says it is time to take her to the delivery room and give her a saddle block. Baggs kisses her and says, "It's getting near twelve."

"Would you like to come into the delivery room and watch?" asks the doctor.

He can't be serious. "That's permissible?" asks Baggs.

The doctor looks at Maggie.

"C'mon, Johnny," she says. "Why not?"

He makes the decision to go AWOL for as long as it takes.

They wheel Maggie away and the nurse gives Baggs a set of hospital greens. He puts on the pants, the tunic, the boots, and the cap, and waits in the hall, dangling the face mask from his index finger. The nurse checks him to make sure everything is fastened and in place. Baggs feels shamed to be unable to pay for all of this, so much more than he planned for. He resolves to pay for it out of the money he has on the books, should they ever find his records and give him his back pay.

A nurse pops her head out of the delivery room and invites him inside. He puts on his face mask and takes careful steps. He is in a sacred place. The doctor, nurse, and anesthetist, however, are merely in their shop.

Maggie, now that she can feel no contractions, is in high spirits. She sees Baggs and says, "What the well-dressed dude will wear."

There is a stool at Maggie's head and Baggs is told by the doctor to sit there.

"Now, if you feel faint," says the doctor, "just quietly leave the room. I don't want you telling me what to do, by the way, and if I should order you out of the room I want you to leave quickly without a word."

"Yes, sir."

Baggs sits on the stool and rubs Maggie's temples. He suspects he is sweating from every pore.

The doctor is at the other end of the table. There is a small mirror above him on a long metal arm. He adjusts it.

"Can you see all right?"

Baggs and Maggie look up to see Maggie's middle framed in the mirror.

When he thought of them, Baggs thought of forceps as being enlarged kitchen tongs that gripped the baby's head like an egg. He is surprised to see they are two long separate implements, each with a rubber grip and a stainless steel base. They remind him of garden trowels. The doctor uses them both at one side of the baby's head to turn him around to the proper delivery position.

It unnerves Baggs to see him stick one in there and leave it as he goes about some other business, but Baggs will not betray himself and get thrown out.

The doctor takes out the tool, which makes a sucking sound as it is removed, and he puts it into a vat of sterile solution.

Maggie and Baggs see in the mirror the wet dark thing. It becomes round and resembles a head. Maggie says, "Oh, it looks like a drowned mouse. Put it back, doc."

"Cool it, Maggie," says Baggs.

"Okay, let's have a push here," says the doctor.

The nurse and the anesthetist bear down on Maggie's belly and Baggs sees the baby pop out like a Roman candle into the doctor's waiting hands. It is a wee thing. Maggie and Baggs are first to see the incredibly large emblems of his sex, free of the sea at last and in the air of earth.

"It's a boy!" cries Maggie.

The doctor passes the baby to the nurse, who brings it closer to Maggie and Baggs.

In pink, black, blue, and red, covered with nature's cold cream, with an oblong head matted with wet hair, shaking two fists no bigger than walnuts, and filling the room with the brass of his first anger and fear, it is a boy.

"My God, ain't that something!" cries Maggie.

Baggs cannot answer. He made the mistake of putting his face mask on upside down and with each of his sobs it threatens to slip off his mouth.

25

THE BABY IS almost too small to be a living human being, thinks Baggs; there have been miscarriages with more beef on them.

Only four pounds and . . . was it six or seven ounces the nurse told him? She weighed it for him as the doctor stitched up Maggie's episiotomy. Parental pride already threatened, Baggs wanted to put his thumb on the scale.

Now she places the baby in the incubator and the tiny fellow falls fast asleep.

"Stir that baby up a little," says the doctor.

The nurse shakes him and he starts howling again. She counts his fingers and toes for Baggs, who agrees that all are accounted for. The nurse makes a hospital bracelet for the new patient. Like father, like son. The baby wears his on the leg, his wrist too small for a dollar cigar band.

Baggs returns to Maggie's head, unable to cease sobbing.

"Do you feel all right?" the doctor asks him.

"I'm just a little overcome. . . . I didn't expect all of this."

"You'll be a good father," predicts the doctor.

"I'm going to try," promises Baggs.

The twins, wakened out of their sleep, practically race across the ceiling when they hear the news. Doug, though he won't smile, is not the coolest cat in Virginia either. He tells the twins to stop behaving like monkeys and he asks Baggs, "What color is he?"

"Well, you won't believe it, Dougie, but he's about six of them."

Baggs describes the newborn baby as they leave the hospital. The twins believe he must have been delivered by Disneyland. Already they make plans to take the multicolored kid brother to show-and-tell.

"He won't *stay* that way," says Baggs.

It puts the damper on the twins.

"Once they bathe him and everything he'll just be his natural color."

"Which is?" asks Doug.

"The same as us."

"Look," demands Doug, "is he a spade or is he a honky?"

"Well, I'm afraid he's a honky, Dougie."

Doug spits into the gutter. He is in an even smaller minority now.

"Black people step on their spit," says Baggs. "They're very susceptible to TB."

"What do *you* know about it?"

"Let's be happy tonight."

"They probably wouldn't be susceptible to it if they could have stayed in Africa instead of having TB slave dealers coughing in their goddam faces."

"Watch your mouth."

"Dougie," says Judy, "why do you always look at the dark side of things?"

"She's right," says Baggs. "We should be happy."

"For what? Another honky mouth to feed?"

"I doubt he's going to cut into your rations. He's no bigger than the palm of my hand."

They board the bus. Baggs has been hoping they would get the same bus driver, that would be fun, but this one is as stony as the bulk of them. They sit far behind him.

116

"When are Mom and the baby coming home?" asks Trudy.

"I don't know. I'm going to visit her tomorrow night and I'll ask. You guys are too young to visit, so what I'll do is come by the place to drop off your chow and then go to the hospital. Are you going to be able to get along alone for a few days? Dougie?"

"Don't worry, I'll keep them in line."

The twins groan.

"I know I can count on you. No ditching school now."

"What's the new baby's name?" asks Judy.

"Mom said I could name him," says Baggs, "but I don't know, I think she should do that."

"Let's name him Randolph," says Judy, "and we'll call him Randy for short."

"No, name him Skippy," says Trudy.

"You better name the kid H. Rap," says Doug.

"I'll mention all of your suggestions to Mom," says Baggs, "but I think she should be the one to decide."

"Okay, then," says Maggie, "I'm gonna name him John Baggs, Junior. He's the only one of the four ever had the right to a J-R behind his name."

"I'm flattered anyway."

It is a pleasure to see the bulge in Maggie's belly gone. After food and the day's rest she looks as healthy as she ever did.

"How's John Junior doing?"

"He's awful small," she says.

"I know, I saw."

"We ain't gonna be able to take him home with us, they said, not for maybe a week, until he's at least five pounds heavy and is okay in the lungs and all. This is standard practice, they said."

Maggie is feeling down about having to leave the baby in the

117

hospital. Her harelip, the most inconspicuous Baggs has ever seen, calls attention to itself by quivering.

"I know how you feel, Maggie; I feel the same way. It'll be a big disappointment to the kids too, but what's best is what's necessary. It would be wrong to take a premature baby like John out of the hospital before he's ready."

Baggs loves referring to the baby as John, as easily as if he'd always been a member of the family. It tickles him to call that baby, no bigger than a seven-cup percolator, by the deep and husky name of John.

"You know what happened last night?" asks Maggie. "The weirdest thing."

"What?"

"Me and the baby slept for a few hours after he was born and then he woke up and they put him at my breast, and darned if he didn't eat just like he'd been practicing or something. I guess I must of been groggy because after he was finished eating I thought he looked up at me and said, 'Can I have my old room again?' "

"His old room?"

Maggie points to her stomach.

Baggs wants to listen to no more of this. He is often made unhappy and sleepless by his own imagination.

"You were tired as can be," he says.

"Sure I was."

"Do you know what I did?"

"Huh-uh."

"When I got back to the hospital and took the elevator up to the ward, I said The Lord's Prayer on the way up. What do you think of that? It came on me without my knowing it."

"Having a baby does funny things to you."

"You're not kidding. I looked in on him before I came in here, and I thought, Twenty-four hours ago he didn't even exist.

118

He's still a stranger to me, yet I would throw myself in front of a train for him."

"And you're not even sure he's yours," says Maggie.

"Don't be naïve."

Maggie takes a sip of ice water through a straw.

"Well, he is yours," she says.

"That's nice to know."

"All you had to do was ask, instead of pussyfootin'."

"Aw, Maggie, I wasn't sure you'd know."

"A woman knows these things."

"Thanks, Maggie."

"You're welcome."

"The kids send their love. They're whirling like dervishes. Doug is going to be sore you picked such an obviously Caucasian name."

"Oh, Doug is always gonna be sore about something."

"He's slow to warm up to a guy."

"You can't argue with a fella's personality."

"I don't suppose he's had the best of times."

"That's no excuse," says Maggie, once again successfully avoiding description of those times, yet admitting they were not the best of times. "What did they say at the hospital?" she asks. "You were AWOL, weren't you?"

"Yeah, I was on report by the time I checked in."

"What are they gonna do to you, Johnny?"

"I'm up for a captain's mast tomorrow. I don't think they'll put the cock to me once I explain the circumstances. This was the first offense for me. Of course, they don't know that since they don't have my records."

"I'll keep my fingers crossed."

"I think they were happy to see me back. Everybody figured I went over the hill. They're halfway expecting me to. Lord knows how *that* would turn out."

119

"You're gonna be shed of that hospital soon, I have the feeling. You'll get shore duty and we can pack up and go somewhere. A baby brings good luck."

There may be something to it, because when he appears at captain's mast and tells his story he is fined fifty dollars, payable if and when they give him his back pay. He was afraid of drawing two weeks' restriction, which would have kept him away from his family when they needed him most.

For two more nights he goes by the apartment to drop off the chow sack before visiting Maggie. He has made a narrow inroad with Doug, appealing to him to teach the baby the tricks of survival.

"This kid'll have it together," Doug promises.

On their way out of the hospital, Maggie says, "It just don't seem fair, going to the hospital to have a baby and coming home empty-handed."

"Last time you came home with two, so it's even," says Doug.

Maggie is close enough to cuff his ear.

On successive nights Baggs watches the news on TV, they have a bite to eat together, and he and Maggie take the bus to the hospital, where they sit close to each other and look through the glass at their small sleeping son, the view frequently blocked by a passing nurse. There is contentment.

Baggs suggests it would do no harm, in a few months when John is strong enough, to take him to the naval hospital chapel and have a chaplain baptize him.

Maggie looks at him peculiarly. "Sure, Johnny," she says, "why not?"

26

UNLESS THERE has been a particularly controversial council meeting or a disaster at sea involving a Norfolk-based ship, the local evening news leads off with the top national story before taking up the continuing story of the continuously dangerous intersection, et cetera.

The twins turn on the set a few minutes after the commencement of the broadcast, and although no geographical points of reference are made, Baggs can tell by the strain in the newscaster's face and the waver in his voice that something wrong has happened at home tonight.

"Spokesmen call it the worst tragedy in the sixty-two-year history of the institution. . . ."

There is a shot of a woman in white being ushered down a corridor by . . . whom? The police?

"The nurse's aide reported to have made the tragic mistake was identified as fifty-two-year-old Emma Walker, who was hired for the job less than six months ago."

She *would* have to be black, thought Baggs sadly, whatever it is she did.

"Saint Mark's has declined to release the names of the dead babies, pending notification of the parents. The death toll is now at seven, with several others reported to be in very critical condition. Those that survive, doctors say, will have suffered some degree of brain damage."

It hits him first in the stomach. He bends forward in physical pain, then jumps out of his chair and yelps like a high-strung dog who is hit by falling leaves and has no explanation for the phenomenon.

Maggie supports herself against a wall. Without murmur or motion she is clearly coming to pieces. The twins cry loudly, looking from her to Baggs. They have no idea what is happening; they were not listening to the TV; they were making Daddy comfortable.

Doug knows. He gets the twins their coats and says to Baggs, "We're going with you."

They all pile into a cab. The cabbie looks at them nervously in his rear-view mirror. He takes them to the emergency entrance of the hospital on his own assumption. They do not pay him, but he does not chase them for it.

They rush through the emergency room and make their way toward the main desk. The lobby is filled with reporters and TV news cameras. Baggs notices network cameras and wonders how they are able to be there ahead of Maggie and him.

Several times someone tries to stop them, telling them an emergency is in progress and no one is allowed inside the hospital. Baggs will not be stopped.

In the lobby a group of reporters surround hospital administrators and doctors and nurses in white. Baggs elbows his way toward them. When they are close enough to hear, Baggs stops to listen. Someone is saying, "No, there is no possibility of this being a deliberate act. It's a simple mistake, with profound consequences. In the storeroom off the nursery are two large metal cans, trashcans with plastic liners. The lids are labeled 'Sugar' on one and 'Salt' on the other. Evidently, whoever had used them prior to Mrs. Walker had mixed up the lids when they were replaced. Mrs. Walker, in her routine duty of making up the formulas for the babies in the nursery, used salt instead of sugar."

"And how many are dead at this time?"

"Eight, at this time."

"Do you expect more fatalities?"

"We're doing everything we can."

"The possibility of brain damage in survivors has been mentioned. . . ."

"I'm afraid that's certainly a possibility."

Baggs and his family huddle together, clinging to each other like a family of lower primates plucked out of the jungle and into an alien environment, hiding their faces in each other's fur and darting their heads out in turn to look around them to see if anything has gone back to normal.

The cameras train on them and the reporters turn their attention to the sailor and his family. Baggs can say nothing to them. One of the hospital spokesmen asks for his name and then consults a memo pad in his hand.

"I'm sorry, Mr. and Mrs. Baggs, your child is dead."

John Baggs, Jr.

Maggie collapses to the floor and the clinging cluster that was their family comes undone. Baggs chooses off a man in white.

What happens next is as much a surprise to Baggs as it is to the doctor, who runs down the corridor, his white gown billowing behind him; as it is to the cameramen, who awkwardly run behind Baggs to get it all on their film.

Baggs has the extra speed of a victim, though he is in fact pursuing. He catches the doctor by his tails and swings him like a bolo. The doctor bounces off the wall and into Baggs' fist, leaving there the imprint of his teeth. That quickly it is over and Baggs has been subdued.

A policeman puts him into handcuffs and hustles him into the tiny hospital chapel. At first Baggs believes it is a sedate waiting lounge. Soon Maggie and the children join him. They are to stay in the chapel until they compose themselves and it is decided what to do with them. The policeman stays with them. He points out to Baggs that it is against the law to assault a doctor in the corridors of Saint Mark's Hospital.

Two doctors and a nurse come into the chapel. They explain hospital routine and the medical consequences of too much salt in an immature bloodstream, one of which may be death.

A clergyman comes in holding his hands together and sits between Maggie and Baggs. It is not the province of man, he reminds Baggs, to question the motives of the Lord. We are but so many grains of wheat in His field. Can grains of wheat question the ways of the farmer? The flower of most splendor withers and dies as surely as the lowliest weed. And one should not forget, he tells Baggs, how many lives have been *saved* in this hospital. Baggs asks him to leave.

No sooner is he gone than a psychologist enters. He describes to them their own states of mind and assures them that under the circumstances their reactions are entirely understandable. Each according to his own personality: the children are bewildered and afraid, Maggie is in pieces, and Baggs has demonstrated displaced aggression. Hardly alarming under the circumstances. However . . . however. . .

Baggs, however, will have no howevers. The psychologist is rudely released.

Doug whips out his shank. He's ready to stab someone, anyone. The cop disarms him in an instant and tells him he is going to forget he ever saw a boy draw a shiv in chapel.

Doug sits next to Baggs and says, "That's about the best punch I ever saw. If you caught him on the windbox, you might have wasted the dude."

Rough outfit, thinks the cop.

The injured doctor comes into the chapel and talks through a pad of gauze he holds to his mouth, assuring Baggs and Maggie that he had nothing whatever to do with their personal misfortune. He was not even on duty in the hospital at the time.

It didn't happen on my watch, so to speak.

"You may not have known this," says the doctor through the gauze, "but surgeons are the largest group of heroin addicts in the country. Not hippies or jazz musicians, but surgeons. No one knows what a surgeon's life is like, even if they ever did try to imagine it. We have the highest suicide rate of any professional group. The highest divorce rate. If you can't turn off your feelings in this business, you can't survive. I once saw a surgeon open up a beautiful fourteen-year-old girl to find her ridden with cancer. He broke down and cried right over the patient. He had to be led away. Last I heard, he was piercing ears for a living.

"I know what happened to your child. I'm as sympathetic as I can allow myself to be, as I dare to be. But you should never attack a surgeon. You don't know what a surgeon's life is like. Last week I had to tell two sets of parents, on the same day, that their small children died on the operating table. Try having a week like that. Last night my kid left the phone off the hook, thinking he could give me a decent night's sleep. At three o'clock in the morning the police were at my door to wake me up and take me to the hospital, where I walked into the operating room and was hit with a stench that you've never had to endure. It was coming from an old man who was literally rotten inside. I found maggots in his ears. What do you think this does to my married life? It destroys it. My wife despises me and I believe she is useless. So do I really deserve a punch in the mouth from you? My God, there were maggots in the old man's ears."

Trudy pulls Baggs' sleeve. "Daddy, what he's saying, is that true?"

"Doctor, you're scaring my kids."

"I'm sorry."

"And I'm sorry too, that I hit you."

The troubled surgeon tells the policeman that he chooses not to prefer charges. The cop adds his condolences to the others and leaves them alone.

No one wants to be first to speak, and they sit in silence for long moments until Baggs rises and opens the door for them.

The cameras are upon them again and one reporter approaches Baggs and shoves a microphone in front of him and says in a low, falsely sympathetic voice, "We know you're going through a terrible ordeal, Yeoman Baggs. Can you tell us how you feel now?"

Baggs looks directly into the camera. The bright lights make the tears come again. His forced smile is the grin of great pain.

"I'm dancing on air," he says.

The reporter turns to the cameraman and says, "We can edit that out, Joe. Mark it. Goddam wiseass."

"Watch your mouth," says Baggs, leading his family home.

What is the weather? Rain, splashing after their ankles as they walk home, like yapping, overconfident Chihuahuas.

27

He is AWOL that night too, but no one puts him on report for it.

The scuttlebutt on the ward is that Baggs' ten-second spot on Walter Cronkite, Baggs' blue back chasing a doctor down the corridor, is sure to cause someone in NAVPERS to wonder just who that sailor was. The Navy is sensitive about public conduct unbecoming. Inquiries will be made. Odds are favorable, in fact, that the commander in chief himself was watching the show. When it is learned, says the scuttlebutt, that Baggs is an unrecorded man without a duty station, someone in a high place will spring him from limbo. What if the competence of the whole naval hospital is called into question?

The XO calls Baggs into his office and assures him that the Portsmouth Naval Hospital is one of the finest medical facilities in the entire world, civilian or military.

"Sir, I believe it is. I just don't want to spend the rest of my life here. It's too hard on my family."

"God's sake, boy, we're working on it. I hope you don't think we've just forgotten you."

Baggs is too tired to worry about the XO's peace of mind. The XO begins progressing through the stations of the clock in his swivel chair. Seven o'clock.

"And I hope you don't think we're an insensitive lot around here. We're all just as sorry as hell for you and your family, and we can almost understand your vicious violence under the circumstances." Eight o'clock, nine o'clock. "I remember some time ago saying several uncomplimentary things about your wife. I want to apologize and take it all back."

"You were right."

"Son of a bitch, Baggs, you sure don't give a person much room, do you?" Ten o'clock.

"Sir, I'm not myself."

The XO swivels to twelve o'clock and looks at the view.

"I was fighting for you today with the old man."

"Huh?"

"I want you to draw some bereavement leave. I assured the old man that, considering the period you've been here, you've got to have leave time on the books. I had to go way out on the limb, though, to convince him you wouldn't take off for Canada or Sweden."

"Sir, I couldn't raise the fare to Newport News."

"Okay, Baggs, you got seven days, starting today. If you're not back here by 2400 of the seventh day, you can give your heart to Jesus 'cause your balls'll be on my key chain."

The XO gives Baggs the chit to fill out and then he signs it, making it official. Baggs comes to attention, does an about-face, and goes to the door. The XO stops him and says, "I know it's godawful the arrangements a fellow has to make in this situation. Stiff upper lip, and my best to your old lady."

They make no arrangements. It is not the money alone that stops them, though certainly everything they don't do is predicated on their lack of funds. Rather, it is Baggs' unwillingness to associate John Jr. with anything other than that tiny screaming multicolored baby with the oversized cock and balls. That is the image Baggs wants remaining in his head, none other. The rest of it he will try to put out of his mind.

So he refuses to identify, he refuses to claim. More than once.

128

His son is sealed in his mind, living again and again his very first minute of life.

The hospital officials are disgusted with him. One woman there has taken to calling him names over the telephone.

He is told that the baby has been removed to the "coroner's mortuary," which changes monthly to give them all an even cut of the business. The state pays for the cremation and begins proceedings against Baggs. How far can the state proceed?

Like a wasted life, Maggie is silent, slow, and dull, always on the edge of intestinal illness. She moves from sofa to chair to sofa, picking at the fabric with her fingernails.

Baggs is able to spend his first full night with her. In the morning when the sun lands upon her face he notices for the first time a thin scar at her hairline. He tries to close it with a kiss. She reeks of Old Sly Fox. Maggie, Maggie, I'm going to love you more, now that you need it more, I promise you I am.

When she awakes she says her first coherent words on the subject.

"I'm glad he's out of it," she says.

"Aw, Maggie, shut up, will you?"

This, even though he's been hungry for some words from her.

"Life ain't no joy ride," she says.

"It wasn't meant to be," says Baggs. Or *was* it? He can't remember.

At last he shares breakfast with the children. Joyless. They won't go to school. They lie about as listless as Maggie.

Though on leave, Baggs must return daily to the hospital for noon and evening chow, his sack in hand, if he wants his children to eat.

He lies awake the last night of his leave, smoking cigarettes. He thinks Maggie is asleep, but finally she calls his name, her back to him. "Johnny?"

129

"Yes?"

"The baby wasn't yours."

He pets her hair. "What makes you think that can make any difference now?" he says.

They throw in their lot with a lawyer who is handling a suit for some of the other parents who lost their babies. This way it costs them nothing and if successful they will receive 50 percent of the judgment, splitting with the attorney. The difficulty in such a case, explains the lawyer, is that a newborn baby is not worth much, legally speaking.

28

THE SCUTTLEBUTT is no more than scuttlebutt. If anyone in a high place has taken notice of Baggs, he has forgotten about him, because Baggs remains in limbo.

Maggie is a long time mending. It might help for her to be out working again, now that she has some figure back, but Baggs has said an end to the bars. A job at the five-and-dime store would be wonderful, but just as some girls are morally incapable of working the bars, others are just as unable to stand all day behind the counter of a five-and-dime store.

Too bad; they could use the money.

The crying begins all over again when they receive a bill from the hospital. But by the time the second, third, and fourth arrive, they are able to take them in stride.

A typewritten note does not move them. An even stronger, more personal note actually brings a dark smile to their lips. They do not know how strong the next letter is; it is thrown away unopened.

A curly-haired man from a collection agency shows up one evening while Baggs is at home. Baggs has him in and invites him to take whatever he pleases. The man sees the threadbare blanket, pillow, and Doug's pajamas on the sofa; he sees the twins asleep on their cots in the kitchen; he sees the fuzzy picture on the battered Philco. He has a few words with Baggs about his financial status. He goes away embarrassed.

Maggie has passed out in the bedroom.

The next night when Baggs comes home, Maggie says, "That woman from the hospital who called before called again."

"Oh?"

"Yeah. She kept saying over and over again, 'What kind of people *are* you? What kind of people *are* you?' "

"Did you tell her, Maggie?"

One evening after sex she says to him, "Did you ever hear anyone say, 'East is East, and West is West, and never the twain shall meet'?"

"Sure, it's from a poem."

"What does it mean, exactly? I'd like to know."

"What do you think it means?"

"Well, I figure it means, you go where you want to and I'll see you if I get there."

Baggs smiles and says, "I have a feeling that's not what the man meant when he said those words."

"So tell me what he did mean. That's why I asked you."

"I think he was only wondering if a Chinese girl could find happiness with a boy from the Bronx."

It is not long before Baggs comes home to see her in the bedroom, putting on her one good pair of pantyhose. She kicks her leg out to the side to get the pantyhose settled right, and then she kicks out the other, like a dancer limbering up, which, though Baggs does not yet realize it, is essentially an accurate description of her preparations.

She has on her sweater that shows the outline of her nipples. She steps into her mini and into her heels. She has done her hair and wears her working makeup.

"I gotta get out of this joint, Johnny, or I'm a dead one for sure."

"The bars, right?"

"It's my cup of tea." She even laughs at last. "Hey, that's not a bad joke."

"Stay here with me, Maggie."

"Don't be a hot dog about this, please. You've never been nothing but sweet with me, and if I ever loved anyone it would have to be you. You're the onliest boy I ever knew had an ounce of character."

"Maggie, your goin' back to the bars is got to put a hurt on us."

How quickly he is back to talking like a sailor now that she is back to talking like a bargirl.

"No, it ain't," she says. "I'll always be cherry with you."

"I got to admit the words didn't mean that much to me when I said them down at the courthouse, but since then something's happened to me. I mean to stick by those promises now."

"Well, so do I, silly. This don't mean I'm running out on you. I only got to get out of this place and we're hurtin' bad for money. You can't say we ain't."

Baggs sits on the edge of the bed. She goes through her purse.

"Will it be the old place, then?" he says.

"Probably. I got to look around and see what's shaking first. I've been out of circulation for so long."

"Don't bring anyone home, Maggie, after midnight."

"C'mon, Johnny, don't start up accusing me already. I don't have even one foot out of the door yet and you're talking about me bringing a boy home after you're back at the hospital."

"I'm going to get out of that place one of these days. Even you said so, remember? We can pack up and go to a new duty station somewhere, all of us. Maybe even to New Orleans."

"That was before," she says. "That's when I thought we was going to have good luck."

He follows her one night. The place has a straight bar longer than a bowling alley. A bouncer like a Brinks truck checks IDs at the door. When he sees that Baggs is beyond twenty-one, he parts the curtain for him and Baggs enters the blue smoky twilight. Here in the Equator Club the Beatles still are and forever will be the cute kids they started out as. "I Want to Hold Your Hand" blares out of the jukebox.

As is his custom, Baggs works his watchband over his plastic hospital ID bracelet and sits at the end of the bar closest to the door. He orders a beer and it hurts him to count out the seventy-five cents for it. The bar is crowded and his back is bumped time and again by sailors and girls arriving and leaving.

His eyes adjust to the dark in a few moments and he looks for Maggie among the other girls at the tiny round tables that surround the postage-stamp dance floor.

He sees her out on the dance floor. He tries to isolate her partner. A sailor, like all the others, like himself. It surprises Baggs to see that she dances so well.

Maggie is laughing, high and raucously, appreciating the wit of her sailor, a real good sport. Pairs of seekers jumping on the dance floor, the sailors looking for free skin, the girls looking for reenlistees about to pick up their shipping-over bonuses.

In his own case, Baggs could at least claim that it took *two* New York City fancy girls to separate him from his shipping-over pay. One way or another, though—two New York City fancy girls or a Norfolk, Va., scag—it all filters down to love or money.

When the music stops, Maggie and a sailor, not her partner, pass on their way to tables. The sailor reaches behind him and grabs Maggie's ass. Maggie swings around, chases him about six steps, and plants a kick. A handful of sailors lower their heads to look up Maggie's skirt as she lifts her leg to kick. The sailor is roughed up good-naturedly by his friends. Maggie, in a mock-indignant huff, marches to her table. She is laughing by the time she gets there, and the sailor she sits with tries to feel her up. Sixty percent trying, forty percent feeling. A waitress stops at the table with a tray of beers and champagne cocktails.

Why don't you go over to the table, Baggs, grab your wife by the wrist, and take her home, in the name of God?

Maggie's her and I'm me, is his explanation to himself. And never the twain shall meet.

He has finished his beer and has no more money for another. The last thing he sees in the Equator Club is Maggie sliding the sailor's cigarette lighter across the table and into her handbag.

Would she believe him if he told her how much she hated sailors?

In the weeks that follow, money becomes less of a problem.

It has never been easy to live with another human being. How easy has it been to be alone?

29

BAGGS DROPS his food bundle on the table and the kids cluster around it.

"Where's Mom?" asks Baggs.

They do not answer him. Something is not right in the Baggs household. He goes to the bedroom hoping to find a drunken Maggie.

Nothing in the bedroom but an envelope bearing his name and pinned to his pillow.

"Good *night,*" says Baggs.

He stands at the bed and looks at the envelope, his hands folded behind him. This is not a grocery list, not a note reminding him of the PTA meeting, of dinner with the Johnsons, of drinks with the Joneses, not a promise of the sweet love she will give him when she returns from her block work for the Junior League. This is a Dear John.

John wonders how a pre-theo from the rural American middle class became head of a family that could be so easily dissolved by a note pinned to a pillow. No marriage counselors, no group encounters, no trial separations, no division of property, no custody hearings. Not even a proper divorce. Only Dear John.

Irresponsibility. Baggs' false idol. A denial of life and love and family in favor of unencumbered motion.

Vanity and vexation.

Here I stand, announces Baggs, and he even widens the space between his feet to stand more solidly.

136

A rush of Biblical phrases come to mind.

Hypocritical nonsense, Baggs warns himself. Lousy egotistical dramatics, he thinks as he reaches for the envelope. It is probably a note of no consequence, and here is Baggs making it one of the major revelations of his life.

> *Dear Johnny,*
> *The children are yours.*

All fears confirmed now.

> *I know you'll be a good daddy. You can change their name if you want to. I am going to New Orleans. Once I get there I know everything will be fine and I hope everything will be fine with you all too. When you get mad at me just remember I was lady enough to write this note. The boy I'm going with said I shouldn't bother, but I told him, well, I certainly am so going to bother. Give the kids a kiss for me. They'll understand.*
>
> *Love,*
> *Maggie*

So much for mom and dad and the home life. Maggie resumes her early existence of eating chicken-fried steak in two-tables-and-a-counter restaurants along the road, a boy she knows picking up the tab.

Baggs without appetite tortures a few beans with his fork. When the children have eaten all the food, he scrapes up the cold and tasteless paste he has made and swallows it. Nothing is wasted.

Baggs is thinking about how to break it to the new orphans, who were so hungry they did not speak of the absence of their mom. How does he tell them that what must pass for parents in their case is one penniless YN2 with no records? How does he advise them to toss themselves at an adoption agency, after their little lifetimes of spooky experiences with agencies and institutions?

It would be best, though, believes Baggs. The twins would be snatched up in a minute by some childless executive and his wife, who would dress them in cute identicals and give them lessons in something every Saturday morning before the matinee. They would have dolls to mother and a real bed to sleep in and a decent diet for once in their lives. They would eat steak, thinks Baggs. He wants to see his little girls wrestle with steaks, instead of always pouncing on cumshaw chow stolen from the naval hospital. It would be best.

. . . But poor Dougie.

Who will take in poor Dougie, a precocious thirteen-year-old half-breed? One look at his rotten teeth and he would be rejected. All the childless executive would have to do is catch a glimpse of the spade's switchblade, and it would be back to the orphanage for Dougie.

Here I stand. Baggs repeats the resolution now that it has real purpose. *Oh, God, my heart is fixed*—Psalm 108. I *will* be mother and father both, I *will* provide, I will *accept responsibility*. I will fix my son's rotten teeth, I will give my daughters lessons in something, I will . . .

Until he makes himself sick with his own sentiment.

He calls the children around his chair. He has carried Edna St. Vincent Millay in from the bedroom. The twins are delighted, they think a story is coming. Doug sullenly comes closer and sits at Baggs' feet with the girls.

He reads the poem without introduction, as though it were not a poem at all. He edits sloppily as he goes along.

> "Listen, children
> Your mother is dead.

From her old coats
I'll make you little jackets;
I'll make you little trousers
From her old . . . huh . . . *jeans.*
There'll be in her pockets
Things she used to put there,
Keys and pennies
Covered with . . . huh . . . *lint;*
Doug shall have the pennies
To save in his bank;
Judy shall have the keys
To make a pretty noise with.
Life must go on,
And the dead be forgotten;
Life must go on,
Though good women die;
Trudy, eat your breakfast;
Judy, take your medicine;
Life must go on;
I forget just why."

It makes no impression upon them, save for a measure of
confusion.

"I don't have any bank," says Doug. "What would I do with
a jive bank?"

"Keys to *what?*" asks Judy.

"I've botched it, looks like," admits Baggs.

"Is Mom dead?" asks Trudy.

"Who killed her?" wonders Judy.

"*Aggggggghhh!*" cries Baggs, dropping to his knees and trying
to capture all three in his embrace.

Why do children in their innocence annihilate so easily? Here
breaks a sailor's heart to know his daughter believes that Mom

could die only at another's hand. In his heart Baggs believes that is the way she will go.

"No, Trudy, no, Judy, no, Dougie," says Baggs. "Your mother is not dead, no one's killed her. Dumb old me thought it was easier to read that poem than to tell you the truth. Your mother's left us."

"Where'd she go?" asks Doug.

"New Orleans."

"She always wanted to go to New Orleans," says Judy.

"That's where I was born," says Doug.

"Big deal," says Trudy.

"So what this means," says Baggs, "is that you're all stuck with me."

"Goody!" cry the twins.

It cuts no ice with Doug.

After the twins are put to bed, Baggs shows Doug the note. "So that's the way it is, Doug. What do you think I should do now?"

"If I were you, I would take off," advises Doug.

"Dougie, you're brutal."

"Practical. You're never going to catch me scrounging around to support three bastards from out of left field. You're not the first boyfriend our mother has had, and you can see for yourself you're not the last."

"I was her *husband.*"

"Now you're not. If you had any sense of survival you'd smash out of here."

"Would you?"

"Didn't I tell you I would?"

"And what if I did? What would become of you three?"

"I would make it. I would survive."

"Doug, all you've ever done was talk about it."

"You don't believe me? Take off, see if I don't. I'll survive. If I have to, I'll eat a rat."

Somewhere in this grim boy's mind there must be the desire to dine on rodent.

"What about the twins?"

"Are you kidding? Chicks sit down on their survival kits."

"Doug, they're only children!"

"Hey, you ever hear of dirty old men? There are some dudes the twins are already too *old* for. If they worked as a team, there's no limit to where they could go."

"I'm ready to slap your face!"

"Don't try it, motherfucker; you'll get cold steel right between the fourth and fifth ribs," says Doug clinically, into his combat position.

Baggs tries to embrace his son, but Doug would rather survive.

30

THE CHILDREN are unaffected by the loss of their mother. The twins prefer Baggs anyway, and Doug is a loner. Baggs himself settles into a numbness which makes it impossible for him to assess his own feelings, except that he thinks she left him too easily to be gone forever. On the other hand, he doesn't believe she will return.

He leaves Doug in charge of the twins and zombielike takes to walking the streets at night. At a coffee counter he is shocked out of his reveries when he sees his eternal love—the girl who married another immediately after he married Maggie—sipping tea with a girl friend. She has not seen him. Should he approach her? Maybe things have not worked out for her either, maybe now together they can return some order to the universe.

He takes tentative steps toward her and notices that a childhood accident has robbed her of an ear. Baggs wants to think it was a childhood accident. What he really concludes is that if he had not looked so closely, she would still have both ears. Who knows what she will lose if he goes any closer? Would Maggie have been so scarred if Baggs hadn't come so close?

He rushes outside to the cold Norfolk concrete, a candidate soon for the nut ward; his children will be scattered, growing up bitter strangers, their memories made opaque.

He is their sole parent and only means of support, and he is still on Cinderella liberty without a pay record. Next time Miss Watkins the social worker visits, the children will be taken away from him. He holds a family conference and asks them if they would like a foster home and three square meals a day. Doug says nothing, but the twins cry to know that Daddy would even suggest such a thing.

He gives them his promise that he will hold the family together somehow. He cashes the last welfare check and writes to the department to discontinue the aid. No more money is forthcoming from any source. They will not starve, thanks to the bountiful galley of the naval hospital, but rent and utilities must be paid, clothes and other necessities purchased. He lies all day on his hospital bed, working out feasible schemes.

He has tried to borrow from the crew of the *Begonia,* his old ship, but the first time he tried the ship was under way and on his second visit he found that the personnel had changed over since he checked into the hospital that fateful day so long ago. The chief has made twenty and retired to South Carolina. Wertz has shipped over for Hawaii, Fisher has extended for photographers' school, and Brown has taken his civilian penis to New Jersey to amaze the assembly line of a General Motors plant there.

Baggs goes to the *Bradshaw* to put the touch on Andy Warwick, his fraternity brother. He carries under his arm a manila envelope so that the OOD will assume he wants Warwick for some official communication.

Andy is angry and embarrassed to see him. He leads him to the fantail, saying, "Are you here?"

"Who, me? No."

"I think you took advantage of me. You never intended to take me on a liberty with you guys. You were making fun of me, and me treating you like an equal."

"You're right. I've been a louse. Andy, it's too long a story to tell, but I've got to get some money."

"You already owe me five."

"I'm going to take you on liberty with me. It'll break your heart."

"You always thought you were better than everyone else."

"That's not true. I just thought you were inferior. I'm sorry."

"Boy, I could have you arrested for the way you're talking to an officer."

"Go ahead."

Baggs does not mean it.

"I'm not that kind of officer."

Lucky for Baggs.

"You never realized you had a good friend in me," says Warwick.

"I have a friend in Jesus," says Baggs, quoting the hymn.

"Him too," says Warwick.

"Andy, I'm desperate. Give me all the money you have. Put it in this envelope."

"You're crazy."

"If you don't, Andy, I'm going to throw you over the side. I'll tell them you made a homosexual advance."

"You really *are* crazy."

But Andy is taking no chances. He empties his wallet. Eighteen dollars. Baggs is sick at heart. Such a grandstand gesture should be worth thirty.

Before Baggs turns to go back to the quarterdeck, Andy says, "Next time you see me you'd better salute, dammit. As far as I'm concerned, we're not brothers anymore. I'm going to write to the alumni president and tell him about you."

Baggs borrows every penny he can from the men on the ward. He goes to two downtown clothiers and opens charge accounts on his ID card and hash mark, sign of the career sailor. He lists his duty station as the USS *Begonia* and buys a thirty-dollar sweater at each store.

He sells the sweaters for twenty dollars apiece to sailors

144

waiting for buses at the Greyhound station. With this and the money he's borrowed he pays off his bill at the two clothiers. Using them as a reference, he opens charge accounts all over town.

In one weekend of mad and glorious shopping he and the kids fill the apartment with merchandise. Among the haul are outfits for all plus Barbie dolls for the twins and a stiletto for Doug. Doug throws it into the door and comes as close to thanking Baggs as complimenting him for his skill in selecting a good blade.

Baggs becomes an after-dark, side-street merchant. Most of the stuff he begins to sell at 50 to 70 percent of original price, but one night he actually sells a pair of western boots for three and a half dollars more than they were worth. After that he adds some polish to his hustling instinct and finds he can sell the goods at an average of 80 percent of price.

He pays the rent, he pays the utilities, he pays off two of the charge accounts and uses them as references to open five more.

He is making a living.

"Hey, gunner," Baggs calls to a passing gunner's mate. "What size shoe do you wear?"

The gunner's mate slows his step and stops when Baggs moves the package from under his arm.

"Nine and a half," he says.

"You're in luck, gunner; I got a pair of nine and a half Hush Puppies. Really comfortable on your feet when you're beatin' the bricks, not like Navy issue. Take a look at 'em."

The gunner's mate inspects them, runs his hand over the material. "These are new," he says.

"Of course they're new. What do you think I am, a junk dealer? These are quality shoes, thirteen ninety-five."

"Too much," says the gunner's mate, about to walk on.

Baggs stops him. "Not for you, naturally. Thirteen ninety-five in a store, ten bucks on the street."

"No way."

"It's my last pair; you can have them for nine dollars."

He leads the gunner's mate into a storefront to try them on.

They settle on seven fifty, and Baggs calls him a thief. Actually, he would have sold them for six.

Into the coffee can, out of which the children get weekly spending money for the first time in their lives. The twins blow theirs on candy. Doug saves to buy his own copy of *Soul on Ice*, though he's already worn the corners off the single library copy.

Now that they are off welfare and have cash of their own, Doug finds fewer people to hate. He even calls Baggs by name occasionally. He never calls him Dad. He still calls him Padre, derisively.

The twins remain constant in wealth or poverty; they hate no one. Even they, however, are hard pressed to forgive whoever left a broken beer bottle in the playground sandbox, where Trudy fell on it and gashed her palm on the jagged glass edge. Baggs made butterfly bandages for the wound and thought, Someday you will lie next to a boy in the morning sunlight coming through the window, and you will say, "Cuts? You wanna talk about cuts? Take a look at this. You get a couple of these babies and blood don't scare you anymore." Baggs kissed the little hand and told her the scar would someday confound a palm reader, and wouldn't that be a good trick on the gypsy?

Baggs himself finds little time for hate. One night he is reminded of Forshay and he is stunned to think how little he's thought of him during the past weeks. He's forgotten to look for him, ask for him. It disturbs Baggs to think he may have given up the search and is doomed to a kind of agnosticism, neither finding nor denying.

What reminds him of Forshay is the twins' singing, " 'M-I-C, see you real soon, K-E-Y, why? because we like you! M-O-U-S-E!' "

Could anyone but another sailor divine his association of the company commander with Walt Disney's contribution to the culture?

Military Indoctrination Company; MIC for short. It was where they dropped the queers, bed-wetters, fuck-ups, and bad boys to give them a taste of what the brig held in store for them. There were three ways out of MIC: the brig itself, an other-than-white discharge, or back to a regular recruit company, fully indoctrinated. There was one other way. During Baggs' stint in MIC, one of the recruits, while marching with the outfit to noon chow, took a nosedive under the front wheel of the old man's limousine.

Forshay waited until the tenth and last week of boot camp before sending Baggs to MIC, which meant that when he achieved indoctrination, which in Baggs' case took two weeks, he would join a new company at Week One and would have to repeat the ten weeks of boot camp. As Baggs suspected, when he was transferred out of MIC he was assigned to Forshay's new company. Fortunately, a month later Baggs came down with pneumonia. When well enough to leave sick bay and resume training, he was transferred into a company whose commander was Saint Francis of Assisi in comparison to Forshay.

In MIC, every night before lights out, the recruits would stand at attention by their bunks and sing, " 'M-I-C, see you real soon, K-E-Y, why? because we *like* you! M-O-U-S-E!' "

A back burner is relit for Forshay, but what becomes Baggs' true adversary is Doug's poor mouthful of bad teeth, each tooth a challenge to his paternal responsibility. He resolves to have them taken care of, he doesn't know how. The money he has put into the coffee can will have to go toward rent because soon the whistle will be blown on his current enterprise. The captain of the *Begonia* has been deluged by dunning letters. These have been forwarded to the executive officer of the hospital, as Baggs knew they would be eventually.

The XO calls him in again and fans out the bills.

"Baggs, you must know that nothing irritates a CO or an XO more than civilians on his back about one of his men."

"Sorry, sir."

"Indebtedness *is* a court-martial offense."

"Yes, sir, I know it is."

"You can get a discharge, less than white. Try and get a decent job with one of those rags."

"I'll take my chances, sir."

"Even dogs won't shit on a dishonorable discharge."

An idle threat. Baggs knows full well they cannot give him a DD. The worst they can give him, if they can discharge him at all, is a general, but the fact is they cannot give him any kind of discharge without records, and the XO knows this.

"Well, Baggs, I'm afraid I'm going to have to restrict you to the ward."

There it is, the worst they can do to him. It is plenty. It would make street urchins out of his children and a nut out of him.

Baggs sobs without pride against the XO's knees, telling him about Doug's rotten teeth. The XO slaps him out of it and helps him to a chair. Baggs worries that he may have overplayed his hand and he watches the door for two corpsmen with a strait-jacket or a hypo.

The session is long, but finally the XO reinstates Baggs' Cinderella liberty, on the condition that he personally does what he has to do to stop the flow of dunning letters.

Baggs goes to each merchant who holds an account on him and explains that he has back pay tied up. He promises to pay

148

in full when his records are found. He signs an IOU for each of them. One sad old merchant invites Baggs behind the counter and shows him a drawerful of IOUs and bad checks.

"This time it will be different," Baggs tells him.

"Yeah, yeah, yeah, this time the river will flow upstream."

What Baggs does not do is return the goods still in stock in his apartment.

31

BAGGS MEETS Doug in the corridor outside the dentist's office. To keep the appointment, Baggs has to miss evening chow at the hospital, but he carries a bag of bread and fruit and envelopes of salt, pepper, and sugar scrounged from the ward's noon chow trays.

"Dougie, why didn't you go inside and sit down, read a magazine?"

"How can I go into a dentist's office? I don't have a dime in my pocket."

"They're not charging admission, Dougie."

"They're gonna charge us *some*thing. You can't pay."

He gives the receptionist their names and they sit with the others. It is a long wait and magazines can fill only so much of it. But it appears they are the last patients of the day. This is good.

The dentist hails them well met and calls Baggs Jack, but the initial reaction of seeing a high-yellow boy in the custody of a uniformed sailor is the reaction that Baggs will cherish.

The open-wide order must be given twice before Doug will bare his molars to professional inspection. Moreover, the dentist must say, "Wider."

Even the miter-joined frontals, out like the cowcatcher on a locomotive, are brown and decayed.

"You certainly haven't brushed regularly," accuses the dentist.

"I bleed when I brush," says Doug, his tongue constricted away from the dentist's probing fingers.

Baggs is in a philosophical frame of mind and at first hears Doug's personal refutation of the proverb *Haste makes waste:* "Ah heed when ah rush."

"I shouldn't wonder," says the dentist, who understands the language and interprets for Baggs.

"Doug, that's terrible. I didn't know."

"How would you know?" says Doug.

"This mouth must be causing you a good deal of discomfort," says the dentist with professional understatement.

"I chew tobacco," says Doug.

"You *what!*" asks Baggs.

"It helps kill the pain."

Dear God, can we ever know the suffering of another, no matter how close?

God only knows where he gets the tobacco.

Baggs puts his hand over Doug's. Doug shakes it away.

"Are you the boy's father?"

"Stepfather."

"Why haven't you taken him to the naval clinic?"

"It's a long story, doc."

Baggs can see the multitude of suspicions darting in and out of the dentist's head.

"I'll make it short. They've lost my records. They have to take care of me because I have a valid service card and a uniform, but the Navy doesn't recognize Doug as my lawful son. C'mon, if the United States can refuse to recognize a whole country or two, even though there it is, right on the same earth, with millions of people running over it, then the Navy should feel entitled to refuse to recognize that I have a son in pain."

The dentist, however, is still on the first line, enjoying the concept of lost records. He is a veteran. He knows. He cannot stop fondling darkly the irony of it. He very nearly chuckles, but for Baggs' benefit he says, "That's ridiculous."

"SNAFU," says Baggs.

"It's a wonder we ever win a war."

"Bureaucratic quagmire," says Baggs.

"The right way, the wrong way, and the Navy way," says Dr. Bouma.

They have used the abbreviated form of the litany, appropriate in the presence of a third, uninitiated party and in the middle of a task to be continued. The dentist has extended his sympathy and Baggs has accepted, yet both know that the dentist relishes its having happened, but not to him.

Now he is ready for business.

He sings out the number of the tooth, the locations and type of rot and probable treatment. Nurse has in front of her a template of the human mouth and as the doctor calls out the cavity, she creates its reflection on her chart.

Baggs looks over her shoulder in growing despair as he sees the thing take form, like a pointillistic portrait. He is jarred when he hears words he recognizes. "Extraction, extraction, gold crown, extraction . . . "

Doug tightens under some of the probings and his eyes water, but he makes no sound. A tough little kid. A survivor.

Finally, the man lays down his tools and Doug has a rinse. The chair is moved back to normal position.

"What is the technical diagnosis?" asks Baggs. He is thinking perhaps he can find a book somewhere. . . .

"Rampant dental caries," Dr. Bouma shoots back, not intimidated. "You want to see another dentist? He'll tell you exactly the same thing: rampant dental caries."

"What do you suggest?"

"He should have a complete set of X rays."

152

"Roger."

"Then the teeth must absolutely be repaired. The quicker the better. Cut out all pop, all candy, sweets of all kinds."

Baggs and his boy share insiders' sighs. Who can afford pop, candy?

"All right, doctor, let's get on it. The lad is at your disposal. I'll write a note to his school."

"You want me to do the work?"

"Naturally. We respect you."

"But you're in the Navy. . . ."

"I explained that."

"Oh, yes, I see. Very well, make an appointment with my receptionist . . . and arrange for payment."

Doug is suddenly interested in the water that swirls constantly around the porcelain basin.

"Ah, the payment. Doctor, there is no money."

"Pardon?"

"I can't pay you. I wish I could. If I could, I would give you as much as you ask."

"It's considerable. The boy needs extensive work."

"Yes, I can see that. You've had your eye in the mouth of poverty here today, literally."

"I'm sorry, Mr. . . . Mr. . . . "

"Call me Jack."

"I'm sorry, Jack, but I must be paid for my services. You must have understood that before you came here. Every man is entitled to a fee for his talents and services."

This man has given it some thought.

"True, but I receive no fee," says Baggs.

"You're the temporary victim of a complex system."

"I'll pay you when the complex system discovers me and gives me my back pay."

"I'd like to help, but you must realize I cannot conduct a practice in this manner."

"Can you turn away this boy whose teeth you've just examined? Can you tell him to chew more tobacco?"

"I'm sorry. . . ."

"Do something wild and irrational for once in your career. Start the work and see if it becomes an uplifting experience for you. See if it makes you feel good to save this boy from his agony. If it doesn't, just discontinue the work and do instead whatever brings you pleasure."

"Mr. . . . " The dentist checks the chart. "Mr. Baggs, I resent your bringing the boy here and trying to put me on the moral spot, when you knew fully well you could not pay."

"Doctor, the kid won't smile. Would *you* smile if you had his teeth?"

"I'm sorry, but would you go into a restaurant and order a big meal and then not pay?"

"That will come, that will come. I've assumed the responsibility for three suffering children, and I'm probably one of the seven least able individuals in the state of Virginia to do it. All I'm asking for is a little bit of help. You know why I'm doing it?"

Doug is certainly interested to learn why.

"It makes me feel good," explains Baggs. "It makes me feel awful, don't get me wrong. I mean, I'm ready to cry at the drop of a hat, but it makes me feel *good*. It's a feeling I want to share with you, doc."

"That sort of thing doesn't work here."

"All right, then. We'll barter, just like in the days of the pioneers. All I have is my body and the hours of four o'clock to midnight. I'll sweep your floor, clean the office, polish your picks."

154

"I have a service that comes in, and they have a strong union."

"I'm a yeoman. I can type and file."

"No class," says Doug in disgust.

"I'm sorry," says the doctor.

"Let me shine your shoes," says Baggs without shame.

"There will be no charge for this visit, but you must go now."

Doug gets out of the chair. He does not wait for Baggs, who hears the door buzz as Doug leaves. He will see later that Doug has swept all the magazines off the table.

"The kid won't smile," he says again.

The dentist is out of his smock. He looks vulnerable for a poke in the guts, but Baggs masters the urge. He doesn't want to fall into the habit.

"Can you recommend another dentist?" he asks.

"Of course not," says Dr. Bouma.

That night Doug challenges him further by putting his fingers into his mouth and withdrawing a dead tooth.

32

SOMETIMES IT helps, but most times it doesn't to see someone even worse off than you are, and you know you're as bad as ever you've been.

They are about to pass each other, the only ones in the arcade that leads from the bars to the bus station. Baggs drifts toward him, a cashmere sweater for sale under his arm.

This man he approaches is not in the market for cashmere sweaters. He is coming out of his shoes and wears a Navy-issue raincoat too large for him, horribly wrinkled and stained. He holds the raincoat at its buttons as though he has something to hide. Some mucus has dried below his nose.

And yet he also drifts toward Baggs. They come together like dancers for the last number. They speak at the same time, Baggs saying, "You wanna buy a cashmere sweater?" and the derelict saying, "You wanna see a skin show?"

Together they answer, neither interested in the other's service, "What kind?"

Baggs takes the sweater out of the brown paper bag. The bum runs the back of his crusty hand along the fabric. "Nice stuff," he says. "You got it in navy blue?"

Something in Baggs begins to boil like leftover soup on the back burner.

"One-of-a-kind item," he says to the crud that stands like a man, and he leads him into the entranceway of a closed shop, a familiar chamber of commerce to both night dealers.

156

"How much?" asks the bum, who puts a hand into his changeless raincoat pocket, pretentious of substance.

Baggs gives nothing for hygiene and fouls his hands on the bastard's neck. As he squeezes, his arms tighten and the gagging specimen rises to tiptoes.

The red, sand-encrusted eyes are popping. The throat wants to say its last: "*Baggs!*"

His saliva runs over Baggs' hands.

"Forshay!" hisses Baggs, watching the company commander's face for the promised change of colors due the strangler in the night.

The pressure of richness and rebirth between the fingers, like a farmer in the earth, a baker in the dough.

"Whaddaya got against *me!*" chokes Forshay.

Hateful people can seldom understand why they are held in such contempt.

Baggs removes his hands and the corpse slumps to the ground in a sitting position, his back against the plate-glass door. Baggs wipes his hands on his pants and turns to go. He hears the breath, like the end of a keg of beer.

He still lives.

Baggs chooses not to finish the job. He starts a kick in the face, but lowers his foot out of simple ennui. The moment is gone.

Baggs neither leaves the scene of the crime nor stoops to make amends. Forshay comes around, rubs his neck, spits a few times next to his knee, and says, "You gotta helluva grip."

"Isometrics."

"What made you stop?"

"Christian charity."

"Ha!" says Forshay, drawing up a knee to rest his arm upon. "If you had any, you'da finished the friggin' job."

"You're a bad man."

"Ho-hum."

"And I hate your guts."

"Hey, listen, let me cry here on the goddam sidewalk for you."

"Watch your mouth."

"You want me to lay down a few tears? Maybe I can knock out a little snot for you. He hates my guts, he says. Ho-hum."

"You disgust me."

"Put in a chit," advises Forshay.

"Why aren't you in the Navy, you eggsucker?" asks Baggs, standing over him.

Now for an instant Forshay looks like the shadow of something human. His soul has been touched.

"I got out," he says, and an honest tear is visible at the corner of his eye.

Baggs will not have compassion for him, no matter what his story. The Navy, such as it is, is better for having Forshay out of its ranks. What happens, or what has happened, to this ugly, emaciated, filthy degenerate is of no human concern. If the Lord should care to intercede, that's His business, but Baggs wants no part of the miserable wretch.

Still, he cannot help looking at him slumped and disgusting on the sidewalk and remember how he looked in boot camp. You could see your reflection in his spit-polished shoes. His piping always gleamed and his blues were free of lint. His white hat was immaculate. He was the picture, physically at least, of the four-point-oh sailor.

"You look like a pile of dog turds," says Baggs, "and you always were so four-point-oh."

The tear in the corner of Forshay's eye loses its hold. "I was, wasn't I?" he says.

In view of Baggs' capital, the charitable donation of a quart

158

of Old Sly Fox is generous to a fault. Curiosity is not a factor, he tells himself. He cannot care less what happened to Lynn Forshay's naval career. The man lost his rights to membership in the human race long before this.

"I got the big old cock put to me," says Forshay, sucking on the bottle and sitting on a crate in the alley behind the Chinese restaurant where he has free office space. He hands Baggs the bottle.

"Don't make me sick," says Baggs by way of refusal.

Forshay takes another deep slug.

"I got busted and dumped and gave a BCD and no pension. Baggs, I gave 'em the best years of my life, dreaming about that pension. I had some dough on the books. I woulda opened a little beer bar here in Norfolk."

His eyes grow misty and he drinks again.

"Well, if anyone ever deserved a bad conduct discharge, it was you," says Baggs.

"You're a candyass, you know that? You always was. Goddammit, I made men outa boys."

"Watch your mouth."

"You think that's easy? You think that don't call for a special talent? What was I supposed to do, give 'em milk and brownies and tuck 'em in? A ship is a team. One shitbird on ship's crew can lose the whole ship in an emergency. I wanted to make sailors I'd be proud to call shipmates."

"Oh, dry up. You enjoyed hurting people."

"Well, I gotta admit it wasn't all long hours and low pay."

The sadist chuckles.

"You went too far one time, didn't you?" guesses Baggs.

Forshay offers him the bottle, but Baggs makes a face. Forshay guzzles another whack of it, wiping up with his fingers what runs down his chin.

"You know the worst kind of boot in a company?" asks Forshay.

"The fag?" says Baggs.

"Yeah, you're right, I forgot about the fags. I wasn't thinkin' of them. I cured a lot of fags in my day."

"You're sick. You can't cure fags."

"Hell, I invented stunts that could cure anything. We had a guy once had a fear of the water. Couldn't swim. I don't mean he had a fear of the water, I mean a *fear* of the water. I blame the recruiter. The recruiter told the shitbird he didn't have to know how to swim and he wouldn't have to go to sea. He was probably behind on his quota and was hot to sucker the guy in. Well, we cured him PDQ of his fear of water, up there at Great Lakes."

"Oh, yeah? How?"

"We threw him in the middle of the pool with his flat hat and his boots on."

"And that cured him?"

"It drowned him."

Baggs thinks it is typical sailor overstatement.

"You don't mean *really* drowned."

"Yeah."

"C'mon!"

"Whaddaya mean, c'mon? We drowned the shitbird."

Baggs covers his mouth with his hand and mumbles to himself. Forshay offers him the bottle again. This time Baggs wipes the mouth of it like a shoeshiner and takes a big swallow.

"What am I *do*ing here," he mumbles, and takes another swig. "What did they tell the kid's family?"

"Whaddaya mean? They told him we drowned the punk. You think the U.S. Navy tells lies? You say that and you better stand up and tangle ass right here and now."

He even tries to get to his feet.

160

A Chinese cook comes out of the back door of the restaurant for a breath of fresh air. He sees Forshay and holds his nose and makes a deprecating sound of recognition.

"Bend over, slanty," shouts Forshay. "I got somethin' for you!"

The cook, still holding his nose high between thumb and forefinger, goes back inside the steamy kitchen.

"Goddam gook!"

"Watch your mouth."

"All the time I been back here in this alley I never seen a scrap of chow. Everything goes back in the pot. This place ain't even on the garbage truck's route." He takes another swallow. "Now, where was I?"

"The worst kind of boot."

"Second worst. The fags are the worst. Once at sea I had a fag on the bridge tell me he had my something-or-other dangling. I told him to hand it over. He whips it out and I grab aholt of it good and I take him for a tour of the friggin' ship, from bridge to bilges. He was scared shitless I would pull it off if he didn't follow me. I even introduced him to the XO that way."

Forshay has a good laugh remembering it and he scratches his scaly ankle. "Now, where was I?"

"The second-worst boot."

"Right. The bed-wetters."

"Bed-wetters?"

"You ever have to sleep below a bed-wetter?"

"I never ran into any."

"That's 'cause we weed 'em out or cure 'em. I cured many a bed-wetter in my day and made a good sailor outa them, so what thanks do I get?"

Baggs is almost inclined to stop him. He almost does not want to hear any more.

"He was a very nervous kid," says Forshay. "He'd stand at attention for morning chow with blood running down his face from the fifteen nicks he gave himself trying to get a close shave. I finally had to get another shitbird to give 'im a shave every morning."

He hefts the bottle with disappointment and has another drink.

"The problem was it took me a while to find out he was a bed-wetter. He kept stuffin' his skivvies and fartsacks inta his locker. One of the other boots reported the smell."

"What did you do?" asks Baggs, afraid to ask.

"Nuttin. I did nuttin."

"You had to do something to get a BCD."

"Nuttin constitutin' cruel treatment. I gave him his piece and covered him with his pissy fartsack and gave him the morning watch on the dumpster."

"What month?"

"It was in February."

Baggs takes the bottle from him and swigs some of the thick sweet wine. He remembers too late to polish the mouth of the bottle.

He also remembers what it was like to stand the morning dumpster watch at Great Lakes in the dead of winter.

A dumpster is a large, iron, fireproof container for trash. There are a number of them on any naval base, but only in Great Lakes and San Diego are they guarded twenty-four hours a day. The guard's duty is to see that no one throws burning trash into the dumpster, that no team of enemy agents steals the dumpster, that no one makes love in (or to) the dumpster.

It was a favorite trick of Forshay's to give Baggs the morning dumpster watch, and then send back his relief to shave a few times or polish his boots or change his skivvy shirt before allowing him to relieve the watch. The morning watch officially begins at 0800, but in boot camp the custom is to get an early chow pass, eat, and relieve the watch by 0645 so that he can get chow. The morning watch is to be relieved at 1145, which makes it a long five-hour watch, but Forshay always managed to make it an hour longer.

Baggs drew the morning dumpster watch on Christmas Day, as he knew he would. The temperature was -16 when he assumed the watch at 0645. By noon it had warmed to -7. The wind sliced across the grinder and through Baggs and through the thick iron of the dumpster, he suspected. It was a wind from the lakes of such consummate brutality and such rocky inhumanity that Baggs concluded the Navy must have originally selected this site to be close to brother wind. It struck you with a chill to shatter your heart and suspend your mind and coax you to dive cheerfully into the fires of hell simply for the rise in temperature.

By 1100 the snot had frozen on Baggs' lip. By 1200 his fingers were locked fast around the butt of his piece. He saw his company go to noon chow and he saw them return. By 1300 his mouth had frozen into a pout, which in half an hour would be his kiss good-bye to life and the Navy.

A friend from the company took a great risk to run down to the dumpster to tell him that his relief had been trying since 1130 to pass inspection, but Forshay kept harassing him. There was no telling how long it would be. Baggs was unable to speak and had only slight movement in his toes. Before running back to the company the friend wished him Merry Christmas and blew a few times into Baggs' face to try to thaw him out a little.

At 1340 Baggs made the decision to lay down his piece and crawl into the dumpster to await either icy death or macabre rehabilitation in the brig. He even made the effort to drop the piece, but was stopped in time by his relief. Baggs had to be helped back to the company, where he was placed in the drying room (120 degrees) until suppleness returned to his mouth and fingers, and his nose ran freely once more. When he was able to speak, his first words were, "I'll find him someday and I'll kill him."

"You put a kid out there in February with a pissy sheet over his head?" asks Baggs and takes another drink of wine before passing the bottle back.

"Good training for a bed-wetter."

"He died, didn't he?" asks Baggs and already his heart is drenched in mourning for the unknown bed-wetting boot.

"Yeah," says Forshay. He sloshes the wine in the bottle. It is a regrettably skimpy portion.

"I changed my mind," says Baggs. "I really do want to kill you."

"You watch your ass. This time I'm ready for you. My hands are like vises. All signalmen have hands like vises."

Baggs grabs his viselike hand and squeezes until Forshay falls to his knees and cries for mercy. Baggs releases him and he crawls back up to his perch.

"I'm losing my grip," he explains, tucking the injured hand into his armpit.

"What am I doing here?" Baggs asks himself again. "With a subhuman like you. You aren't even fit for this back alley. You belong in . . . in . . . the *Navy.*" Baggs is amazed at this conclusion, which contradicts his earlier opinion that the Navy was better for the loss of Forshay. "You really do, you know. Civilian society is not ready for you. You're ahead of your time. You belong to the military society. You're the lowest . . . as low as . . . ."

"I'm one of the lowest things in the world," confesses Forshay. "What my mother has been all her life, which is one of the reasons I never liked her."

"What?" asks Baggs, eager for an apt comparison.

164

"A civilian," says Forshay, who wraps his head with his arms and adds, "without a pension."

"The kid is dead," Baggs reminds him.

"It was politics."

"Everything is," says Baggs.

"I'm a political exile."

"That's what they all say. What's your story?"

"Aw, the kid's old man was an unsuccessful candidate for governor of Delaware. *Dela*ware! And only an unsuc*cess*ful candidate. Shit fire!"

Now seems a good time to leave. Baggs no longer needs revenge. It has been a long, tedious journey, but he has arrived. Simple curiosity moves him to ask, "What are you doing now?"

It takes a bit of warming up, a drink, and several preparatory gestures before Forshay can mumble, "Hustlin' for a skin show."

"Women and police dogs? Sixty-nining? Lesboes? That sort of thing?"

"Yeah, that sort of thing."

"*Ecccchhh!* You in the show?"

"I was, sure, but did you ever see the thing on me? Everybody laughed. Besides, I couldn't keep it up. Sex is finished for me. If I never have to do it again I'll be happy. I'd be glad to be a monk, if they asked me to."

"Why don't you kill yourself, Forshay? Take a walk in the woods and let the wild animals have a meal out of you. I don't see that you're much good for anything else."

"Fuck you, Ditty Bag. You got a brother? Fuck him too. Don't look to me like you come too high in the world either, hustlin' hot sweaters."

"I got three kids to feed."

"And you talk about me being messed up? At least I don't have no kids to hang around my neck."

"They may be hanging around my neck, but they're hugging me at the same time. I got someone to say hello and good-bye to me. What do *you* have? You don't know what it's like to go into an apartment at night and have three people who love you. Two anyway, the twins. I'm never too sure about Doug, but I love him so it's the same difference. If you knew what responsibility was all about, you wouldn't be the revolting thing you are. If you ever had a kid to love you, you wouldn't like to hurt people."

"Oh, look at who's gonna tell me about responsibility. Look at who's tellin' an SM1, Regular Navy, about responsibility. What rate did you finally get, by the way?"

"Yeoman second class."

Forshay slaps his legs and roars. "A cunt! I shoulda knew! If somebody ever came up to me and said, 'Remember Ditty Bag? What do you think he struck for?' I woulda said yeoman, quick as lightnin'. Well, I guess the Navy got four years' use out of your dainty fingers anyway."

"I'm still in," says Baggs.

Forshay is astounded. "You shipped over? You?"

"Yeah."

"That's because you had me for a company commander. Somebody you could look up to. I bet lots of my boys shipped over."

"I'm going to barf on your lap," says Baggs.

"What ship are you on?"

"I'm on temporary duty at the Portsmouth Hospital. Temporary forever. They lost my records."

Forshay chuckles. "That's terrific. You wonder how they do it. I think what happens is some pussy like you drops them in a confidential burn bag and they get torched. There was a boot at Great Lakes once, they lost his records and he spent four years there, and then he lost his mind. He used to ride a motor

166

scooter to chow, only he didn't have no motor scooter. Was always honking his horn at pedestrians."

"Well," says Baggs, rising, "all good things must come to an end, and fortunately so do bad ones. I'll let you get back to your perverts and police dogs."

Forshay grabs him by the arm. "I hate that kind of life!" he cries. "Once I stood tall, in the service of my country."

Baggs shakes out of his grip. "Suffer. It's getting late. They only give me Cinderella liberty at the hospital and I want to go home first to say good night to the kids."

"You got a place to stay? I don't got a place to stay tonight."

"Oh, man . . ." Baggs has fallen downwind of him. He smells fecal. "When was the last time you had a bath, you pig?"

"Hey, look, I didn't come here to be insulted by a cunt who don't have as much time in the Navy as I have in the goddam *chow* line."

"Watch your mouth."

"How about taking a big kiss offa my ass?"

Baggs wonders if a good open-hand slice at the throat would do it cleanly and forever.

33

Baggs takes Forshay home. He doesn't know why, and yet he does know why but is deliberately slow to face it. To face up to his current view of the world would be to admit to insanity.

On the face of it, it is justice that Forshay is out of the Navy, because Forshay is not altogether human; on the other hand, what better place for him? Anywhere else and he would be at odds with his environment.

Doug helps Baggs prepare a bath for Forshay and together they lower the frail naked white and yellowing body into the tub. Even the pubic hair harbors debris.

"Ahhhhhh!" Forshay sighs, out of memory made real again. "Ahhhhhh!" as he slides down to the chin. "You're all right, Baggs. I always said that."

"We call him Padre around here," says Doug, "a selfless seeker of poverty and redemption."

"Bull," from Baggs. "Whatever I do I do for me."

"Then why did you bring this bum here?" Doug asks.

"Why do you think I did?" As though it were obvious. It seems obvious to Baggs. Does he grow more mad the longer his records are at large? Will he soon go speeding breakneck down the hospital corridors on his imaginary Vespa?

"Face it," says Doug. "You don't have the stuff to survive. While you're back in the ward, this bum will steal what little we have left and maybe just strangle the twins and me in the bargain. I'll have my shank in hand," he tells Forshay, "and I know how to use it too. I'm half black."

"You're Baggs' kid, all right," says Forshay cryptically. He breaks wind underwater and is amused by the feat.

Doug and Baggs stand back, elbow to elbow, watching the bath water darken from Forshay's filth.

"Forshay," announces Baggs, "how would you like to be back in the Navy?"

"You shouldn't even bullshit about something like that," says Forshay with sorrow like a goiter.

"Forshay, what do you want out of life?"

"Only what I had: three squares, a dry fartsack, and the uniform of my country, which is proper dress for any occasion in the world. You going to a fancy-dress ball? All the guys are in tuxes and tails? Well, your Donald Duck suit is jake. They *gotta* let you in."

Forshay sighs, remembering dignity and the way really to live.

"You got it," says Baggs.

Forshay puts both hands on the edge of the tub, unable to speak.

"You're going to be me. You ever hear about the chow in the hospital?"

Forshay rivets his head enthusiastically.

"Three times a day for you, rain or shine. Nothing to do all day but swap sea stories and play cribbage and Monopoly and watch the tube."

"Oh, sweet Jesus!" is Forshay's response to the description of heaven.

"Nobody busting your hump and it's open gangplank every night if you want to come downtown for a beer."

"Open gangplank," says Forshay, as if long overdue for a night on the beach.

"Cinderella liberty, of course."

"Look, midnight is late enough for any man to be out by himself. What's right is right."

Scratch your head, Forshay, you're a nigger too.

"Forshay, YN2, do you swear to uphold the Constitution of the United States, to . . ."

"Cut the shit, kid. Hey, what about this YN2 business? I don't know a typewriter from a hot rock."

"Chances are they'll never find your records. . . ." (Already they are *his* records.) "Chances are you'll spend the rest of your life on that asshole ward. . . ."

No objections from Forshay. "Good duty," he points out.

"But if they should find your records"—Baggs breaks into a large grin—"you'll find you got money on the books."

"How much?" As though it matters. If you're on a good feeder and a good liver, money's only good for shooting craps.

"Few grand. It's yours, YN2 Baggs."

Forshay is out of the tub, wetly trying to embrace Baggs.

"You brought home an old faggot," says Doug.

They give him a towel and as he dries, Baggs says, "If they do find your records and give you duty somewhere, just put in a chit for change of rating, take the test, and go back up on the bridge. Yeomen are a dime a dozen, but a good signalman is hard to find."

"And I'm one of the best," says Forshay.

"I'm going to brief you for a few days on the setup, get you a uniform out of the lucky bag, we'll exchange cards and papers and that'll be it. At midnight you'll check in and forever after you'll be John Baggs and I'll be Lynn Forshay, God forgive me."

170

A whole new set of sins to atone for, but Baggs feels up to the task.

Doug clears his throat.

"Dougie?"

"I can't help pointing out," says Doug, "that Forshay looks ten years older than you, about five inches shorter, maybe forty or fifty pounds lighter. He's got different hair, different color eyes, and there is absolutely no resemblance in the face."

"They ain't gonna notice I'm not you?" asks Forshay, his dreams already in jeopardy.

"So what if they do? They don't have any records! If somebody says you're not Baggs, deny it. Let them prove you're not. They can't do it! What's more, they probably won't want to! One Baggs is as good as another to the good old USN. All you have to do is say a few times a day, 'Did you find my records yet?' That'll convince them you're me."

Baggs gives his surrogate the marriage bed and returns to the ward.

34

A FEW NIGHTS later Baggs comes home at six-thirty with a heavy case under one arm, a brown paper sack under the other. He will tell no one what is in the case, like a child with a surprise, but in the sack is a uniform for Forshay.

Forshay lays it out on the bed and lovingly runs his fingertips across the wool. He shakes out the neckerchief to see if the previous owner knew his business. He twirls the white hat on his thumb.

"Try it on," says Baggs.

There are some private preliminaries in Forshay's mental apparatus before he strips to the skivvies. The twins giggle on each other's necks at the sight of his skinny white legs and the stencil on his skivvy shorts: WADE, over which some master-at-arms has stamped the red DC which indicates that the discarded clothing in question is in the public domain.

Forshay steps into the trousers and fastens the thirteen buttons. The jumper goes over his head, and lo, he is upright and half a foot taller. He arranges and ties the neckerchief, and his sneer returns from drydock. He positions his white hat at eyebrow level. Here comes the arrogant swagger, in bare feet.

He cups a hand against his nose and announces, "Now, hear this, now, hear this, there will be no liberty until the morale improves."

Baggs, Doug, and the twins all snap to attention and salute smartly.

"It's spooky," observes Doug. "There must be some word in

psychology for it. Like, I know this kid who's a roller skater. He's probably the best in the country. I watch him out on the rink and it makes you catch your breath. Poetry in motion, like they say. But the minute he takes off his skates and tries to walk he turns into a sniveling, nail-biting dope that no one can stand to be around. He drools and trips over his feet and can't string three words together. But on a pair of skates he could lead you into hell."

"Hey, Sambo, blow it out your ass," says Forshay, guessing at the parallel.

They spend the evening reviewing what they have been drilling into Forshay: the physical layout and SOP of the hospital, the names and characteristics of the nurses, corpsmen, and men on the ward, Baggs' serial number, personal background, and previous duty stations.

At eleven-thirty, like a note in a bottle, Forshay is tossed off on his own.

There is no sleep in the Baggs—belay that—*Forshay* household until middle morning comes without the bootfalls of SPs in the hallway. They look at each other and say cautiously, "Well . . . so . . ."

The twins are tucked into their cots in the kitchen and kissed night-night. Baggs stops by Doug's couch on his way to a few sleepless hours of his own. He sits on the coffee table to say good night to his son. He is deep in the blues of the newly made civilian, like the parolee who shudders to realize that prison was also home.

"It's going to work out fine," he assures his son to assure himself.

"I'm not so sure," says the realist. "I know *I'm* going to be all right."

"Relax, Dougie. I'm going to take care of you now, you and the twins. You know what happened today? I got a job."

173

"With a salary?" asks nobody's fool.

"Salaries are for rank-and-file bums. I'm a lone wolf."

"Your brother's at the door."

"Dougie, Dougie," sighs Baggs, "you had no childhood."

"Among other luxuries," says Doug.

"You win, Doug. Now give me some slack, will you? I'm going out into the real world tomorrow and I'm going to come home with money. I promise you that. If I don't come home with money, I won't come home at all."

"You don't have to jive up an alibi with me. If you want to take off, take off. I would if I were you."

"I'm sorry, Doug. I didn't really mean that; it was a figure of speech, a proud boast. Of course I'm going to come home tomorrow. You poor kid, is that what you're worried about?"

"Don't put on airs. Who cares if you come home or not?"

But if no one cares, then why does Dougie have to flip over on his side and shove his face hard against the backrest?

It is a pale and shaky Baggs who lugs his sample case in the morning to the bus stop, the new man on the territory. The twins, as usual, are spastic with excitement and good wishes. Doug, as usual, guards vigilantly against the lifting of spirits.

The Baggs who returns at six o'clock is a good actor auditioning for the part of Willy Loman. His face carries gloom like a rash. He lowers his case in the corner and lowers himself to the case and lets his hands dangle between his knees.

The twins bite their knuckles; Doug dons his shades.

"Maybe now you'll learn," says Doug.

"What?" asks Baggs.

"That the world is a shitpile and you're at the bottom of the pile."

"Is that so?"

The girls do not recognize the change in his tone and Trudy says, "We love you anyway, Daddy."

"Doug, remember what I told you last night?"

Doug cannot believe it. Has Baggs brought home money?

"You bet I have!" says Baggs, rising and casting off his disguise. Willy Loman, hell. Sammy Glick. "All the money in the world. Forty bucks! Yeah, that's right, forty big ones. I cornered all the dough in town. What's more, I'm going to do it every day. I want everyone in this apartment to know that he's got forty bucks a day coming in, six days a week, except for the weeks I feel like working seven. Got that?"

It is out for dinner that night, and they fall upon steaks like savages, roaring and carrying on so gleefully that none of the other patrons can object. Chocolate sundaes for dessert, and Baggs almost weeps over his coffee to learn that he has given his children their first meal in a restaurant.

"You've never eaten out, not once?" he whispers.

"Not so you could sit down at a table," says Judy.

"We'll eat out again tomorrow on my second forty bucks," says Baggs.

"We'll pay some rent," says the new bookkeeper.

"Doug's right," says Trudy. "We can buy food at the super-market now."

"You know what I'd like to do," says Baggs. "I'd like to save up enough for a down payment on a car. We'd take a vacation and drive to New Orleans and look up somebody we know there and show off a little."

"Why bother?" asks Doug. "She'll be back soon enough."

"Who?" ask the twins, playing dumb.

At home, when the girls are asleep, Doug demands to know Baggs' line of merchandise. He will not be put off, though Baggs tries.

Finally, Baggs kneels with Doug at the black case and he opens it for inspection.

The Book of Life.

Doug takes a volume and opens it like a good librarian, from both sides, gently flattening the pages, working toward the middle to ease the stiffness of the new copy. *The Book of Life.* He looks at a color plate of the Lord.

"It's so perfect I think I'm going to be a little sick," says Doug. "The Padre is spreading the word."

"Just trying to make a buck," insists Baggs.

"You made forty dollars selling these today?"

"Why not?"

"How? How did *you* con anyone into buying this stuff?"

"You like cake, Doug?"

"Huh?"

"Sure you do. You love it. Boy, would you ever love Biblical cake."

"Biblical cake?"

"A taste of heaven," says Baggs. "You want the ingredients? Well, just take the same number of cups of brown sugar as the number of sons Zebedee had with him mending their nets. Add eggs, the same number as days Paul stayed with Publius at Melita. Take the number of camels Abraham's oldest servant took on his journey to find Rebekah as a wife for Isaac, then subtract the number of letters in the name of the apostle to whom it was said, 'Behold, an Israelite in whom is no guile!' and you got the number of cups of sweet milk. Cups of flour, just take the number of loaves divided by the number of fishes when Jesus fed the five thousand."

"Wait a minute," says Doug. "I happen to know it was two fish and five loaves. Right? That would be two and a half cups of flour, two into five goes two and a half. It *was* five loaves, wasn't it?"

"Oh, was it?" taunts Baggs. "Add the number of years Joshua lived to the number of years old he was when he was sent by Moses to spy the land. Subtract the number of fishes the

176

disciples caught at the sea of Tiberias, and you got the number of teaspoons of baking powder. Then it's simple. All you have to do is take two cups and put as much lard and butter into each as what Herod swore he would give the daughter of Herodias. Don't try to remember it all, I have it written down."

Baggs takes a sheet from his sample case and hands it to Doug.

"This is the stroke of genius that separates Baggs from your ordinary *Book of Life* salesman," says Baggs.

Doug looks at the puzzle and says, "It's the stroke of *something*, Baggs."

But he remains on his knees and starts leafing through the index, one eye on the recipe for Biblical cake.

Baggs is too keyed up to sleep and asks his son if it's all right to take a walk, maybe have a beer.

Baggs opens the door, but Doug detains him. The Great Stone Face is at last smiling. The hell with rotten teeth; a smile is a smile.

"Try to be home by twelve, Pops."

Baggs turns quickly and shuts the door, too pleased to look at his boy a second longer.

35

FORSHAY RIDES the elevator to the seventh floor. He makes a right and déjà vu takes him to the medical station at the entrance to the ward. The nurse, an ensign, looks up from her paperwork as Forshay signs in at the clipboard on the counter. She nods a greeting and goes back to work.

Forshay counts the beds to his right and stops at number five. He opens the night cabinet and reaches in for Baggs' hospital gown. His hand lands on the Bible, which makes him as uneasy as the handshake of a gentleman. He lays it down on top of the cabinet and finds the gown and toilet kit. He repairs to the head to get ready for bed.

At reveille the chow cart is rolled in and he gets up with the other long-timers to help the corpsmen distribute the trays.

He sits on his bed and eats—not breakfast like a lousy civilian, but morning *chow* like a sailor. His neighbor sits facing him and says, "How're you doing, hoss?"

"Four-point-oh, Smitty, how about you?"

"Hurtin' for certain."

After chow he follows the sweepers and swabs the ward with Baggs' swab.

He follows some other ambulatories to the TV room, where he bums a smoke and sits down to cribbage with a sailor who extends his hand and says, "Jones."

"Baggs," says Forshay, pumping his hand.

Jones cocks an eye. "I thought Baggs was that other guy."

"No, I'm Baggs," says Forshay.

178

He beats the kid at cribbage.

The signal is given that the doctor is on his rounds.

Forshay waits at bedside. The doctor pauses at the first bed, looks at the two lines of beds, and tightens his face.

"Good morning, assholes and elbows, if I've got bushels I've got barrels, take your pick. Son, would you take an incisive canal cyst on a trial basis?"

"Not me, sir, thanks anyway."

"Quick as a whip, aren't you?"

When the doctor is at the man next to him, Forshay pulls up his gown and gathers it to his chest. He lowers his face out of sight to his arms on the bed and listens to the voices of the doctor and his aide.

Forshay is sweating at the palms and he feels the tickle of rivulets running down his arms from his armpits. Finally the moment arrives and he hears the corpsman say, "Baggs, sir."

"What would you say if there came a troop of suprasellar cysts a-knocking at your door, Baggs?"

"I'd say, 'I gave at the office,' sir."

"Don't even unlatch the screen door."

"Did they find my records yet, sir?" asks Forshay. What the hell.

But the doctor has started his professional humming and does not answer. Forshay feels the cheeks of his behind spread farther apart and he hears the doctor say crisply to the corpsman, "Right. Let's schedule this lad for surgery tomorrow morning."

ABOUT THE AUTHOR

DARRYL PONICSAN was born in the coal-mining town of Shenandoah, Pennsylvania, in 1938. He has had varying experience in the Navy, as a teacher, and as a social worker, and is now a full-time writer. He lives in Ojai, California, with his wife and young son.

73 74 75 10 9 8 7 6 5 4 3 2 1